Outbreak

ALSO BY MELISSA F. OLSON

NIGHTSHADES SERIES
Nightshades
Switchback

BOUNDARY MAGIC SERIES
Boundary Crossed
Boundary Lines
Boundary Born

SCARLETT BERNARD SERIES
Dead Spots
Trail of Dead
Hunter's Trail

DISRUPTED MAGIC SERIES
Midnight Curse
Blood Gamble

The Big Keep

OUTBREAK

MELISSA F. OLSON

A TOM DOHERTY ASSOCIATES BOOK
NEW YORK

This is a work of fiction. All of the characters, organizations, and events portrayed in this novella are either products of the author's imagination or are used fictitiously.

OUTBREAK

Copyright © 2018 by Melissa F. Olson

Cover images from Getty Images
Cover design by Fort

Edited by Lee Harris

A Tor.com Book
Published by Tom Doherty Associates
175 Fifth Avenue
New York, NY 10010

www.tor.com

Tor® is a registered trademark of
Macmillan Publishing Group, LLC.

ISBN 978-1-250-17629-5 (ebook)
ISBN 978-1-250-17630-1 (trade paperback)

First Edition: June 2018

Outbreak

Outbreak

Prologue

OVERCAST SKIES OR NOT, Corbin Sloane was fading.

He had been following the massive van for more than two hours, and daylight was now seeping through the windshield and driver's side window, hitting his exposed hands, face, and neck. At first, the cloud-filtered sunlight just made his skin tingle, but as time wore on it began to burn. His body began directing energy toward healing, which eventually drained him. This must be what humans felt like when they tried to drive after an all-nighter.

But Sloane wasn't about to pull off the road. He had spent the last two years of his obscenely long life following a young woman named Reagan, a shade who somehow attracted the loyalty of other shades. Sloane, who had spent over a century hurting people for money, surprised himself by falling in line after her.

And, if he was being honest, falling in love with her too.

Unbeknownst to him, however, Reagan had gotten herself involved with shade royalty. Sloane had only learned about it the previous evening, after he saw Reagan shoot Hector's twin sister, Sieglinde, with some kind of dart gun.

For the first time ever, Sloane had been angry with her. No, he was *livid*. They had argued as they drove away from the Switch Creek police station, going round and round. Reagan was tired of being isolated and making shit up as she went along. She wanted shades to have a true leader, and Hector had proven himself willing to lead. Sloane, for his part, tried to point out that Hector was a cold-blooded killer, of both shades and humans, and insisted that Reagan should trust his own experience with Hector over her gut feelings.

Reagan had countered that he, Sloane, had killed shades and humans during his mercenary days too, and that was pretty much when they went back to the starting point. It broke his heart to do it, but Sloane finally gave her an ultimatum: walk away from Hector or he would walk away from her.

And she chose Hector.

So Sloane walked away. Or rather, he drove away, in a gorgeous Bentley owned by a wealthy woman in her late forties who was charmed by his British accent—and the shade saliva he put into her bloodstream. Sloane had driven straight toward I-90 south, intending to cross into Indiana—he had no intention of staying in the same *state* as one of the royal twins—and then make his way south to Atlanta, or even southwest to New Orleans. He had never been to the Big Easy, and it was one of those cities that was so clichéed as a vampire hangout that he was curious to go.

His fantasies about the French Quarter lasted for exactly forty-two minutes before Sloane found himself pulling off the highway and slamming his fist down on the plush leather dashboard. "Goddammit, Reagan," he said aloud.

Then there was nothing to do but turn the car around.

When he made his way back into Chicago, it was easy enough to pull the Bentley behind a state police car and mesmerize the trooper into telling him that Reagan had been captured, alive, and was going to be held at the state police station—Jail? Barracks? Sloane didn't know the American terminology—overnight. Sloane wasn't lovesick enough to walk into another police station full of humans, so he got the trooper to tell him which exit was used for prisoner transfers. He managed to find a parking spot down the alley, where he could just make out the discreet door. And he waited.

The Bureau of Preternatural Investigations in Washington had a few live shade prisoners, so they would be aware that shades were at their weakest shortly after dawn. Sloane was guessing the prison transport would leave shortly before the sun came up, so the shades could get inside the vehicle on their own power, and he was right: At 6:45, just before dawn, a very nondescript, very large van pulled up to the exit, and he saw them come out: first, five armed troopers, wearing those modified hazmat suits that were beginning to spread through law enforcement, the ones that protected cops from shade saliva. Then the three shackled shade prisoners, followed by another five troopers.

Reagan was at the front of the prisoner line—she would have insisted—followed by Cooper and Aidan, her most recent recruits. Cooper, a huge man who had been transmuted in his forties, kept his head bowed, defeated. Aidan was looking around with frank curiosity, neither afraid nor confident. In a way, this was just another day for him.

Reagan, for her part, shuffled along with her head held high, her eyes flashing rage at anyone who looked her way. She was fierce, but Sloane knew her well enough to recognize the slightest slump to her shoulders, a certain resigned sadness in her body language. The last residue of Sloane's anger dissolved when he saw that. She had trusted the wrong person, and she knew it.

He wanted to go get her right then, of course, but there was a whole police station's worth of cops right behind her. Sloane would never have survived for so many decades if he couldn't be patient. He watched as the three shades were loaded into the enormous van and made to lie down in what looked like airtight body bags, made of some sort of coated canvas or leather. Sloane's lip curled. He could see the practicality, of course, but it seemed inhuman.

Then again, that's what the police thought of shades. That's what *everyone* thought of shades.

Once Reagan and the others were secured, four uniformed state troopers climbed into the back of the van with massive guns. Sloane winced a little. Well, he supposed four was better than ten. Two more men came through the exit. Sloane didn't know the younger guy, who headed for the passenger door, but he recognized the older man behind the wheel as part of the Chicago BPI team.

And now, two hours later, he was following the van south on I-90, through the narrowing clog of early morning commuters and around the curve of the Great Lake. As soon as he was certain they were taking the shortest route to Washington, Sloane hung back a few cars, letting a sleek black Hummer H6 take the spot behind the van, where it would hide the Bentley from sight. He had filled the Bentley's tank before he started the stakeout, but he hoped the van would have to stop to refill, somewhere out of the city. The fact that some shades could be outdoors during the day wasn't well known; the cops wouldn't be expecting him to attack in broad daylight.

He'd left too much space in between himself and the Hummer; now a red pickup truck with a trailer inserted itself in the lane between them. Sloane wasn't worried—as long as he could see if the transport van got off an exit, he was fine. His thoughts returned to possible scenarios for an attack. Six cops was a lot for one shade during the day, and he didn't really want to kill them. If he could catch them by surprise . . . and if Reagan could stay awake long enough to distract them . . .

Sloane found himself snapping to attention. His subconscious had noticed something . . . what was it? There: two lanes over, a second black Hummer had accelerated past the Bentley. Now it was moving right, crossing to get closer to the first Hummer . . . and to the transport van. Two identical black Hummers in Michigan? Unlikely.

Before he could even consider the problem properly, a third Hummer suddenly braked in the far left lane, where it had been hidden from Sloane by a semi.

"Bollocks," Sloane said out loud. The enormous vehicles converged on the transport van, which looked small for the first time. They were just coming up on an exit, and the Hummer to the left of the van swung sideways, forcing the van off the steep embankment.

The professional part of Sloane's brain was unimpressed—if he'd been running their operation, he would have gotten subtler vehicles in different colors—but then it struck him who the Hummers had to belong to. He only knew one shade who would make this bold of a move against the government, and he was far too arrogant to buy cars in different colors. He *wanted* the world to know he was involved.

Hector.

Fear shivered through Sloane. He wasn't afraid of much, but the sociopathic king of vampires truly scared him. And it was one thing to discourage Reagan from helping Hector, but another thing entirely to actively move against shade royalty.

But this was Reagan.

Sloane braked as the van tumbled down the embankment, flipping over three times before coming to a rest on its roof, well out of sight of the highway. The Hummers bumped their way down the steep hill, surrounding the downed van. Sloane stayed at the top, pulling the Bentley over and waiting. He opened the glove box and retrieved the weapons he'd stashed earlier: two Berettas and a hunting knife.

Three drivers climbed out of the Hummers, and Sloane could instantly tell from their movements that two of them were shades. They were pale and a little drawn-looking—the sun had been out for hours—but old enough to move with unnatural grace and speed. The third driver, the human, hung back, weapons in hand, while the other two approached the van.

The poor cops never had a chance.

It didn't even occur to Sloane to go help them. Instead, he waited until the shooting started, and then he slipped out of the Bentley and belly-crawled down the embankment, using the scrubby fall brush for cover. No one paid the least bit of attention to him. One or two of the troopers must have rallied enough to return fire, because a stray bullet caught the arm of the Hummer's human driver, who screamed out a curse and fired back. There were still plenty of gunshots in the air, so Sloane raised his own gun and shot the human clean through the head.

Then the gunshots stopped, and there was a long moment of stillness—the shades were probably feeding from the fallen cops. Sloane took a more secure position behind a clump of young pine trees and waited.

One of the attacking shades got out and came over to his human colleague, cursing as he saw the body. After a moment of staring over it, he shrugged to himself and went to the Hummer, opening the massive hatchback before backing the vehicle up to the back of the mangled transport van. He began pulling out tarps—and Sloane shot him in the head too.

The shade dropped. He could heal from that, but Sloane's attention was already drawn to the second shade, who leapt out of the van like something out of a horror novel, his eyes vamped out and blood running down his chin into his shirt. The shade had put everything into the jump, probably assuming from a distance that Sloane was a human, and as he flew toward him Sloane casually lifted the muzzle of his Beretta and shot him in the stomach. The shade let out a very undignified gurgle and tumbled to the ground, blood erupting from his wound.

Everything was suddenly still. Both of the shades could heal from the gunshots, given the amount of blood they'd probably absorbed from the police, but the second one had seen Sloane's face. "In for a penny," he muttered to himself. He raised both Berettas, aimed at major arteries, and fired into the two downed shades until the guns clicked empty.

When the bodies finished jerking, Sloane was fairly certain they were both dead, but he wasn't about to take any risks. He retrieved the hunting knife and went to work sawing off their heads.

Only then, when both heads were fully detached from

the bodies, did Sloane open the back doors of the van.

Reagan was waiting for him.

Someone must have undone her chains—either the state police had removed them after sunrise, or the shades trying to capture her for Hector got the keys. Either way, Reagan was free to leap into his arms, wrapping her legs around his waist and causing Sloane to let out a surprised "oof." He staggered a few steps to be under the Hummer's hatchback door, out of the sun.

"You came for me!" she said, her voice shaky and a little surprised.

"Of course I did, love."

Reagan buried her face into his neck. "I fucked up."

"I know." He could have stood there all day holding her, but she needed to get out of the daylight. Gently, he bent forward a little so she would lower herself to the ground. Her face was pale but feverish, her long dark hair matted in clumps. Her eyes were filled with red, as were his own, and blood was sprayed over the front of both of them. Sloane pushed the hair out of her face, and color and humanity slowly bled back into Reagan's eyes. "We have a lot to talk about," he told her. She nodded, regret on her face. He tilted his head toward the two airtight body bags, which had to contain Aidan and Cooper. "But for right now, we need to find you lot a place to hide."

Chapter 1

LINDY'S BROWNSTONE
LATE FRIDAY NIGHT

SPECIAL AGENT ALEX MCKENNA was about three hours past complete exhaustion, but he lay awake, staring at the ceiling of a vampire's bedroom.

"You okay over there?" Lindy asked. He rolled over to look at her. She was lying on her side, wearing nothing but a sheet pulled up to her waist. Her head was pillowed on her hands, arms covering her breasts. A small smile played on her face, but there was a trace of nervousness, too.

"Yeah. I'm okay. Just . . . wow."

"Dear Penthouse," Lindy intoned. "I never imagined I'd sleep with a vampire, but tonight all my dreams came true . . ."

Alex threw back his head and laughed. "I wouldn't say I've been dreaming of sleeping with a vampire. I was more just wanting to sleep with *you*."

"Was it what you expected?" Lindy asked.

Alex reached over, playing with a loose strand of her blond hair. Lindy was one of the oldest and strongest shades on earth, but at the moment she looked lovely and vulnerable and... human. *So* human. No wonder shades had gone so long without being discovered.

He had almost lost her earlier in the night. The shade they'd been pursuing, Reagan, had shot Lindy with a dart of methamphetamine, which had short-circuited her system. When Alex found her, for a few terrifying minutes he'd been certain she was dead.

"Yes and no," he said. "I was a little ... mmm ... apprehensive. About keeping up with you."

Now it was Lindy's turn to laugh. "You watch too many movies."

"Well, yeah, probably. But it was ..." He was too embarrassed to continue, so he amended, "It was really nice."

She rolled her eyes. "Talk about damning with faint praise."

Alex leaned over and kissed her. "Thank you," he told her when they finally broke apart.

"For sleeping with you?"

"For trusting me."

Lindy pulled away then, sitting up with her back to him. "Alex..." she said after a long moment. "I haven't told you everything."

"About what?"

"About my brother."

Now he sat up too. "Okay . . ."

She looked at him over her shoulder. "There's something you should see."

Lindy stood up, sliding into a robe, and Alex pulled on his boxers and followed her across the bedroom to a closed door that he had figured for a closet. There was a bureau next to it, and Lindy opened the top drawer, dug around, and produced a little key. She unlocked the door, flipping a light switch just inside. Then she stepped back so Alex could get through. "I'll give you a minute," she said, not meeting his eyes. "I need to feed the cat anyway."

Curious, Alex stepped past her into a large closet or small dressing room. It was empty . . . but three of the walls were covered in thick brown paper, the old-fashioned kind that was still sometimes used to wrap parcels. And every single bit of paper was covered in information, like an enormous flow chart.

At the center of it all, facing straight to the closet door, was a letter-sized photograph of Hector. It was grainy, obviously a blowup of a very old photo . . . but the BPI didn't have a single picture of Hector.

Lindy had been holding out on him.

"Jesus," Alex muttered. He stepped closer. There was a thick black marker line leading from Hector's photo to a small sketch of a woman he recognized: Giselle, the shade who had attacked one of his agents and killed many others. Lindy had written "DEAD" underneath the sketch.

But there were many others: lines upon branching lines leading to sketches and photos and scraps of newspaper. "It's a whole goddamned network," he muttered.

Lindy padded back into the bedroom, closing the door behind her to keep the cat out. She'd heard him, of course, and came to look over his shoulder. "These are all the shades I know who have ever worked for him," she said, pointing to the web of faces. Then she gestured toward the top of the brown paper, where a line of dates and descriptions went most of the way around the room. "This is a timeline of his activity, as much as I know."

Alex spun around to look at her. "Why didn't you tell me?"

"I was going to. But I was waiting until you were out of the hospital—I didn't want you trying to go after him until you were better. And then you went to DC, and there was never enough time . . ."

"Bullshit," he spat. "You could have told me before any of that. Or Chase, or Bartell, or any of the others. Hell, you could have put this together at the office, where everyone else could be working on it too. Why did you want to keep us out of this?"

Her eyes narrowed and she stepped closer to him. The metal tracking bracelet on her wrist jangled faintly as she reached up and poked at the thick scar tissue on his shoulder where Hector had sliced diagonally across his body with a knife. She wasn't very gentle about it. "*That's* why. You almost died the last time you went up against Hector. I didn't want to risk you. I didn't want to risk *any* of you." She looked angry, but her voice trembled, and Alex realized she was afraid. For him.

"So why show me now?" he demanded, not ready to let it go. "Because I slept with you and you feel guilty?"

Lindy flinched. "Okay, I probably deserve that," she allowed. "But no. Bartell said something to me last night, about how trust and loyalty need to go hand in hand." Hesitantly, she reached up and laid her hand on his cheek. "You've got my back, and I've got yours. But we're not going to get any further if I don't trust you."

Alex felt the anger dissolve. Lindy was a shade; she'd been hiding from law enforcement for hundreds of years. Of course her perspective on working as a team would be different. "I could have told you that," he grumbled, but he reached over and squeezed her hand. His eyes traveled over all the new possibilities, the new data. It was an investigator's dream, and Alex felt real hope rising inside him.

"First thing in the morning," he said at last, "we're taking this to the office." The next day was Saturday, but Alex would be working anyway, filing endless reports from the day's many events and checking in with the team transporting captured shades to Camp Vamp. "No more secrets."

"Agreed."

He turned to face her. "I didn't know you could draw."

A tiny, infectious smile bloomed on her face, and she tugged on his hand, leading him back toward the bed. "I have many hidden talents."

Chapter 2

LINDY'S BROWNSTONE
SATURDAY MORNING

ALEX STARTED AWAKE, smelling Lindy's lavender and vanilla shampoo on the pillow next to him. Lindy herself was hurrying out of the bedroom, and it was only as he squinted at her departing figure that his brain processed what had woken them up: a banging on the front door. He checked his watch: 8:15 a.m. Shit. He had wanted to be at the office by now.

Out in the other room, he heard a familiar voice talking to Lindy: Chase Eddy, his best friend and second in command, was asking for Alex in a panicked tone.

Alex located his pants where they'd been discarded next to the bed and tried to hop into them while stumbling out of the bedroom—definitely not a great plan, especially before coffee. As he lurched into the entryway, Chase and Lindy both looked at him.

"Hey, Chase," Alex said, wincing. He glanced down at his own bare chest and just-buttoned pants. "This . . .

well, this is exactly what it looks like."

"It doesn't matter." Chase began pacing, his hair sticking out at all angles and his unbuttoned dress shirt flapping over his jeans and a T-shirt. "Why aren't you answering your phone?"

"I didn't hear it. And I thought we had things under control for the night."

Chase seemed to deflate, and he sank down into one end of Lindy's sofa. "Yeah. About that."

Then, as Alex and Lindy listened, Chase laid out the story: he'd realized the week before that he was missing time, and felt compelled to keep it from everyone.

For a second, Alex didn't understand what his friend was trying to tell him, but then he got it: Chase had been mesmerized.

Before the implications could even sink in, Chase added, "I got this idea that by keeping my missing time a secret, I would help protect you from her."

Alex stared blankly for a moment, until Lindy touched his arm. "The easiest way to mesmerize a human is to play on an emotion that's already there."

Alex nodded, feeling suddenly weary. "Protecting me is pretty much part of your genetic code at this point, dude."

Chase let out a broken laugh. "Except I didn't. Or I thought I was, but it was all fuzzy, and someone kept sort of erasing their tracks, and I couldn't keep anything in my *head . . ."*

Oh, God. "That sounds pretty sophisticated," Alex said, looking at Lindy. She stared back at him in horror, and he could read the thought on her face even before it echoed in his mind.

Hector.

Chase knew everything about the BPI, about Alex, about their work with Lindy. He was a perfect target. Why hadn't Alex seen that? Why hadn't he anticipated this, goddammit?

But he knew his best friend well enough to know that there was more. "Chase, what happened?" Alex asked, trying to stay calm.

"Gil called me this morning, when he couldn't reach you," Chase whispered. "The van left at six a.m. Forty-five minutes ago, they were attacked. Harvey Bartell is dead, and so is the kid that Gil sent with him. The shades are gone."

Alex sagged. Bartell. One of his team was dead. Because of Alex's orders.

"Oh, God." Lindy looked as stunned as Alex felt. "Alex, you need to call—"

But his cell phone was already beginning to buzz in his pocket. He looked at the screen: the deputy director of the Bureau, Marcia Harding. Alex's heart sank. "Hang on, I've got to take this." He touched a button. "Hello, Deputy Director. I just heard about the van."

There was an exhalation, then the deputy director's voice said, "I'm sorry to say it, but we have bigger problems than that right now, Alex. Camp Vamp was just attacked. All the inmates have escaped."

Alex was momentarily stunned into silence. Lindy, who was close enough to overhear, clapped a hand over her mouth, her eyes widening. Then she leaned over and whispered an explanation in Chase's ear. Alex forced himself to sound calm. "Casualties?"

"Six, including Lucien Tymer. We need you here."

Tymer had been part of the old guard, one of the few current agents who had served under Alex's mother, the first female director of the FBI. "Me?" He couldn't keep the surprise out of his voice. Chase, who looked like he might throw up, stepped closer to Alex, putting his ear near the cell phone. Alex increased the volume so he could hear too.

"What about Ellen Dawson?" Alex asked Harding. The senior agent in charge of the New York BPI pod was hours closer than he was.

"Alex . . ." Harding's voice was heavy. Alex had known her since he was a little kid. He hadn't heard her sound so disconcerted since his mother's funeral. "We think there was a leak out of your office."

Alex's eyes flicked over to Chase, who had gone even paler. "Oh?"

"I'm sorry. I'm suspending the Chicago pod until we can sort out this mess," she said. "I want you to come to DC and help with this thing."

"Why?" Alex began, but then he understood. Alex was the most famous agent in the BPI. He wasn't just an FBI legacy; his team had also solved the two biggest shade cases to date. "Never mind, I get it. Optics." It had come out more sour than he intended.

"Like it or not, you've become the face of the BPI," Harding said sternly. "We'll talk about it more when you get here. Call your people, inform them that the pod is suspended, and then call my assistant. I'll have her book you a flight. And, of course," she added, like it was an afterthought, "I'm sending Gil and his SWAT team to pick up Rosalind Frederick."

Next to him, Lindy recoiled. "Wait, what?" Alex sputtered. He was about to ask why, but then it was all too obvious: until a few hours ago, Lindy was the only known free vampire in America. She had access to BPI agents, and she could control humans with her saliva. Of course they would assume she was involved in the jailbreak.

Beside him, Lindy must have reached the same conclusion, because the look of surprise on her face quickly settled into irritation.

"Her involvement in this is a disaster waiting to happen," Harding was saying. "But if we can keep it quiet and feed her to the press as a suspect, it will help temper public reaction to the prison break."

"With respect, Deputy Director, I'm not sure that's the right call," Alex tried. "I trust Lindy. And she's still our best hope of catching Hector."

"According to *her*," Harding countered. "Remember, Ambrose fed you Frederick's name. By her own admission, Hector is her brother. What's to say she wasn't playing you this whole time?"

Lindy shrank back from him, looking like she'd been slapped. When she turned her gaze to Alex he could tell she was worried that he was going to believe Harding's new theory.

It hadn't even occurred to him.

He pointed to her bedroom and mouthed the words, "Get the paper." She gave him a questioning look, but then she nodded and rushed toward the bedroom. To Harding, Alex said, "I understand what you're saying, Deputy Director. When is Gil picking her up?" He looked around for his shoes and keys.

"Any minute now." Chase, who had heard most of the conversation, ran to the front door and began peering through the window blinds. In Alex's ear, Harding added, "Our research from Ambrose suggests shades are at their weakest shortly after sunrise, but Agent Palmer isn't taking any chances. He's bringing a full team." There was a pause, and when she spoke again her voice was severe. "I'm sure I don't need to tell you not to call and warn her."

"No, no, I won't do that," Alex said, truthfully. He definitely didn't need to call Lindy.

"Good. Come find me the moment you arrive in DC."

"Yes, Deputy Director."

Alex hung up the phone and looked at Chase, who was peering sideways through the glass. "Three SUVs just parked on the next block," he reported before Alex could ask. "Two minutes, tops."

Lindy appeared at his side, dressed in a simple sundress and flats, with a leather purse crisscrossing her body, a denim jacket strung through the straps. There was an expensive-looking sunhat on her head, making her look like a rich college kid about to hit the farmers' market. Her arms were filled with bundled-up brown paper.

"They'll have both exits covered," Alex stated. "Is there another way out of here?"

She gave him a *duh* look. "There are four more. The roof is our best bet."

He nodded. "Give me your arm." Understanding, she shifted the bundle of papers to one arm and held out the wrist with her bracelet: the unbreakable metal bracelet that served as her own personal federal monitor.

"You sure about this?" Chase murmured. Lindy and Alex both looked at him, and the other agent reddened. "I mean, no offense. But you're throwing away your career here."

Alex met Lindy's eyes. She was weaker with the daylight: less physically alluring, slower, more vulnerable. But her eyes blazed with fierce intelligence, and he could see her running the calculations, her expression softening. "Alex, maybe—"

"No," he interrupted her. "You've got my back and I've got yours." He turned her wrist over and pulled it close to his face so he could make out the tiny, sophisticated lock. The bracelet may have looked like expensive jewelry, but the actual locking mechanism wasn't that different from the kind of combination lock used for bicycles. His brow furrowed, Alex slid in the code: 0918. The bracelet fell to the wood floor with a heavy *thunk*. Lindy immediately rubbed her wrist, the papers in her arm making little crumpling noises.

"Alex! Out of time!" Chase yelled from the window.

"Let's go." He started to move her toward the stairwell, but paused when he realized Chase wasn't following. "Chase?"

"You guys go," he said. "Turning myself in will buy you time."

"Chase—" Alex started, but his friend cut him off.

"*I did this.* Just go."

Alex hesitated, but Lindy grabbed his hand, yanking him toward the staircase. He reluctantly stumbled after her. Over his shoulder, Lindy said to Chase, "Look after my cat. And don't turn yourself in. We might still be able to use you."

Chase waved them away. "No promises, but if I get loose I'll meet you at the White House at four."

Alex nodded. "Good luck, brother," he said quietly, and then he raced up the stairs after Lindy.

Chapter 3

LINDY RAN UP THE two flights of stairs to the top floor of the brownstone without speaking. She was too busy berating herself. Of *course* this was happening. Of course it was. What had she expected? She'd agreed to work for the Bureau of Preternatural Investigations. And now they wanted her to take the fall for Hector's actions.

Maybe she deserved it.

Lindy pushed the thought away before she could fall into it. The brownstone had three stories, but she had a contractor renovating the top two floors. She rarely went up here. They ran up the creaky wooden steps, past wads of industrial-strength plastic and discarded plywood, to the third floor. Lindy led Alex down the hall to a spare bedroom with an access hatch in the ceiling. The building had a small attic for insulation, but it ended before this bedroom. "This isn't on the city's blueprints," she said breathlessly. This soon after dawn, she was at more or less human strength. "I had it installed along with the construction"—Lindy grabbed an old-fashioned wooden ladder that was propped horizontally against the wall—"but I haven't gotten around to installing a lock. Can you open it?" Alex, who had a good six inches of height on her, jumped up, smacking the hatch so it flopped open, filling the room with daylight. Lindy was ready with the ladder, maneuvering it in place. It was redwood—lightweight, but strong—and it was four feet longer than the eight needed to reach the ceiling. She'd had it specially made for this.

Below them, they heard raised voices. Lindy instinctively froze. "That's Gil's team," Alex said urgently. "Go!"

Lindy scrambled up the ladder and onto the roof. Heavy gray rain clouds hung ominously over the Chicago skyline, which was one small mercy. The sun could eventually burn Lindy's skin even through the cloud cover, but it would take hours longer than direct sunlight. Alex popped out right behind her, and helped her lift the ladder up behind him. He closed the hatch, looking around frantically. "Something we can set on it?"

She shook her head, adjusting the wad of brown paper so it was easier to carry in one hand. Her long-term plans had included putting a marble bench on the roof, but she hadn't gotten that far yet. "There's nothing up here. It'll take them a while to find the hatch, though, and by then we'll be gone."

"How?" Alex asked, looking at the deserted roof. Her brownstone was one of four that were connected to each other, side to side, with their entrances facing west.

"They'll be watching the fire escape. And Palmer's smart enough to expect us to run across the connected roofs to the neighboring buildings."

"Trust me." Lindy had chosen her house's location very carefully. With her free hand, she picked up one end of the ladder, and Alex followed her lead and took the other. They jogged south to the roof of the connecting brownstone, which formed the end of the group of four. Just east of her cluster of brownstones, there was another cluster that faced a street over, so the two clusters stood back to back. Alex realized what she was doing and peeked over the edge and sideways, toward the back door of Lindy's brownstone.

"Four agents posted by the door," he reported in a low voice. "I don't think they saw us, but what if they look up over here?"

"No shadows today. No reason to." *And we don't have a lot of other options,* she added in his head.

Slowly, they stretched the ladder across the short divide between the back of the brownstone next to hers and the back of the next building, making a bridge. It fit perfectly, as it was supposed to. Lindy pushed out a breath and stepped to the edge of the ladder, papers still in hand. It was a forty-foot drop below, and she didn't know if she could heal from that, at least not this soon after dawn. She'd probably survive, but in agony—and in police custody. "We better go fast, though."

With that, she got a firm grip on the bundle of papers and ran nimbly across the wooden ladder. When she turned around, Alex was gaping at her. She waved impatiently for him to follow and spoke into his mind. *Come on.* He moved up to the edge, and she thought, *No, don't look down. Look at me.*

He met her eyes, looking a little exasperated, but he stepped out onto the ladder bridge, just taking quick glances to make sure his feet hit the rungs. Haltingly, he made it most of the way across before he started to wobble. Lindy reached out and grabbed his hand, helping him across.

The roof of this brownstone had a small ledge around it, forming a sort of fenced-in patio area. Lindy pulled the ladder quietly over to their side and tipped the redwood ladder up against the inside of the ledge, where it blended perfectly with the reddish brown painted stucco.

"You rehearsed this," Alex said in amazement.

"Of course I did." *You don't get to be my age without having backup plans.*

With Alex at her heels, she ran across the garden patio to the wrought-iron fire escape on the south side, close to the east wall. Lindy thought of this route like moving a knight in chess: two brownstones south, one brownstone east.

Once they reached the street, North Wells, it was a

short walk to North Avenue, which was bustling with pedestrians on their way to the farmers' market. Alex put his arm around her and they disappeared into the crowds.

Chapter 4

LINDY'S NEIGHBORHOOD
SATURDAY MORNING

AT ALEX'S REQUEST, she led him to the nearest drug-store, a few blocks away. Alex grabbed three cheap disposable phones. "Do you have cash?" she asked as they approached the register.

"Only a little," he admitted. "I wasn't really planning to go on the lam today."

"It's really more of a weekday thing," she said agreeably, reaching into her small purse. Glancing around, she handed Alex a thick wad of folded bills.

"Jesus." He shoved the money in his pocket.

Lindy grinned at him. "I, on the other hand, plan to go on the lam every day."

They went out to the parking lot, where Alex insisted they get underground and Lindy pointed in the direction of the nearest subway entrance. He looked a little surprised that she wasn't arguing with him, but Lindy was already feeling fatigued from the escape across the rooftops. She had nothing to prove by hanging out in daylight.

As they began strolling along the street, Alex fumbled with the wrapping on one of the phones. "How's your memory for phone numbers?" he asked her, looking a little sheepish.

Lindy rolled her eyes. "Let's just say it's better than yours." She recited Hadley's number, and Alex placed the call. If she leaned in just a little, Lindy had no problem hearing both sides of the conversation.

"Hello?" Hadley sounded groggy, and Lindy remembered that she'd been up most of the night helping guard shades at the state prison.

"It's me," Alex said. "I'm calling to officially inform you that the Chicago BPI pod is suspended pending inquiry."

There was a long pause, and for a moment Lindy thought she'd fallen back to sleep. "Jill?" Alex asked, probably wondering the same.

"I'm here. Hold on."

A male voice mumbled something in the background, and there were some rustling sounds, probably Hadley getting out of bed and going to another room. Lindy and Alex exchanged a glance. "Faraday?" she mouthed to Alex. He shrugged, but gave a little smile.

Hadley came back on the line. "Boss, what's going on?" she asked.

"I can't get into it on the phone," Alex said. "You

should know that I've been instructed to report to Washington immediately."

Hadley could read between the lines. "Okay . . ."

"But if you're interested, rendezvous point three in two hours," he said. "No electronics."

There was another pause, and then Hadley said simply, "I understand." She hung up the phone.

Lindy waited while Alex had more or less the exact same conversation with Gabriel Ruiz—minus the male voice in the background. Then Alex handed her the cell phone he'd just used, and Lindy obligingly snapped it in half and tossed it into the nearest trash can, asking, "What did that mean, 'rendezvous three'?"

"That night that Hector kidnapped you, the pod set up several potential rendezvous points, in case we were separated or attacked and couldn't call for help," he explained. "The first two are down near Heavenly, but number three is in Orland Park."

"Do you think they'll come?" she asked. "It's not gonna take Harding long to figure out you're not on your way to DC. She might call them."

"Well, that depends on how good Chase's story is," Alex replied. "And I don't know if they'll come. I wouldn't really blame them if they decided not to." He sounded calm, but Lindy could tell he was worried. "But it's the best I can do."

Chapter 5

CHICAGO FBI OFFICE
SATURDAY MORNING

SPECIAL AGENT GIL PALMER still wasn't sure why *he* had been chosen as the Bureau's liaison to the Chicago BPI pod.

In fact, he sometimes lay awake at night reviewing his actions from the months before it happened, trying to figure out where he might have drawn his superiors' attention, in either a positive or a negative way. There was certainly nothing in his background or case history that said: "I want to help fight vampires." He was good at his job because he appreciated the value of grinding away at a problem until it was worn down to nothing. Unlike many of his fellow agents, Palmer didn't even mind doing paperwork at a desk for part of his time. Overall, Palmer thought he was a perfectly average agent who had elevated himself with hard work.

But the world had shifted, and then so had the ground beneath Gil's feet. If he'd been just a little more self-aware, Palmer might have realized that his dependability and steadiness were exactly why he'd been picked for the liaison position, but he was too busy scrambling for his bearings to consider it.

Besides, it wasn't like he'd really gotten a chance to settle into the new responsibilities: Hector had started kidnapping teens only a few months after the Chicago BPI pod was formed. Gil found himself immediately besieged by questions and odd scenarios: How could you kill shades in a hostage situation? How would you contain or transport them? What if you had to fight them at night, when they were at their strongest? And, just this morning: how did one put together a strike team to capture a shade alive?

It didn't help, of course, that he sort of knew the shade in question. Gil Palmer was one of two people in Chicago, outside the BPI pod itself, who knew that the new consultant was a shade. He'd been extremely uneasy when Alex McKenna brought Rosalind Frederick onto the team, and even more uncomfortable when Frederick had gone around and mesmerized all of Gil's agents to forget that they'd seen her fight.

But *he* remembered. God, he remembered. When Lindy had fought against that other female shade, Giselle, it had been one of the most terrifying and awesome things he'd ever seen. Not "awesome" as in "that's so cool." Awesome as in "wrath of God, fuel of night-mares" kind of stuff. The battle—and it was a *battle*—had been a maelstrom of flashing blades and flying blood, punctuated by both women taking the occasional gun-shot as though it were nothing.

And now he was supposed to go arrest the *winner* of that fight?

But orders were orders. Gil still held out hope that Lindy would go quietly. She scared the shit out of him, but in his gut, he just couldn't see her murdering FBI agents.

On the other hand . . . couldn't she have mesmerized him to think that?

At the Bureau headquarters on Roosevelt Road, Palmer told his strike team about their mission to capture Lindy, which was a difficult conversation in itself. His guys felt betrayed, and he couldn't really blame them. At the same time, most of them had secretly been dying to apprehend a shade, and they were convinced they were ready. In less than an hour, Palmer's team had scoped out Lindy's address and parked their SUVs a block away.

They all took a minute to put on face shields and gloves, and then Palmer sent a large group of agents around to the back of the building, and a few more to-ward the fire escapes. When everyone was in position, Palmer took a deep breath and approached the front door, with five more agents at his back.

To his shock the door actually swung open as he walked up, framing a different BPI agent. Chase Eddy gave him a broad, slightly confused smile and opened the door wide. "Hey, man," Eddy said, taking in the strike team behind him. "What's going on?"

Palmer was thrown. Again. In his radio, he ordered the back door team to stand by, then said, "What are you doing here, Agent Eddy?"

Eddy's smile faded. "You heard about the prison break in DC?"

Palmer nodded. "And the carjacking with the prisoners. We're here to pick up Rosalind Frederick."

Chase's brow furrowed. "So am I. I mean, Alex called us both into the office, and Lindy left her car there last night. I'm the closest, so he asked if I would stop and pick her up. But she doesn't seem to be home. The door was unlocked when I got here." His eyes widened. "You think she was involved?"

Palmer studied him. He didn't know Eddy well, but the other agent seemed twitchy and upset. Was he nervous because he lied, or just agitated about the shade attacks on the BPI?

"I was ordered to bring her in," Palmer said simply.

"Well, she's not here."

Palmer took out his miniature flashlight and stepped

up to Eddy. He knew from his conversations with Tymer that there were no quick tests to find out if someone had been mesmerized with shade saliva, but the pupils were *usually* a giveaway. Eddy understood this, because he held still as Palmer shone the lights in his eyes.

Pupil reaction was normal. Palmer relaxed just a tiny bit, and Chase stepped so he was sideways in the doorway. "Come on in and take a look around," he said, still looking unconcerned. "There's a cat around here somewhere, probably shouldn't let it outside. If Lindy's innocent she'll be pissed."

~

He may not have been the most out-of-the-box thinker in the Bureau, but Gil wasn't stupid. Fifteen minutes later he found the hatch to the roof and called for Chase Eddy.

"Did you know about this?" he asked, gesturing to the door, which one of his guys had flipped open.

Eddy looked genuinely surprised. "Nope."

"She was prepared to run." Palmer gestured around the room. "But there's nothing in here to even boost yourself up. No ladder, not even a table."

Eddy shrugged. "There's construction up there; maybe she hadn't gotten around to adding furniture yet. Or maybe she was planning to jump straight up?"

"I don't know if shades can even do that during daylight." Palmer squinted up at the opening, thinking it over. "Me, I would keep a ladder in this room and pull it up after me as I ran. Slow down whoever might be following."

"Did you check the roof for a ladder?"

"My guys are doing that now." Palmer glanced past Eddy. Now that they'd cleared the brownstone, the other agents had split up to search for information on Lindy's whereabouts. It was just him and Eddy in this room. "If there's anything you want to tell me, Agent Eddy, now would be the time."

"Like what?"

"Like you heard about the raid and decided to come warn Miss Frederick beforehand?"

Eddy didn't look particularly offended, more . . . curious. "How would I know to do that?"

"I'm not sure." Palmer gave him a hard look. "But I'll be requesting your phone records to check."

"Go ahead. I haven't been on the cell this morning, and if you check the GPS, you'll see that I arrived just a couple of minutes before you did."

"Except for Alex McKenna's call," Palmer broke in.

Eddy's expression flickered. "What?"

"You said Alex McKenna contacted you to pick up Miss Frederick."

"Oh. Right."

Palmer was about to ask Eddy to hand over his phone, but just then one of his strike team members, O'Reilly, appeared in the doorway. "We've got something, boss," she said, holding up two large ziplock bags. Each one contained a cell phone.

"Two of them? Are they both Frederick's?"

O'Reilly shrugged. "They're password protected. We'll get the techs looking at them."

Palmer pulled out his own phone. He'd programmed in the phone numbers for the BPI pod the day he'd taken the liaison position. He hit Frederick's number, and one of the two phones lit up, vibrating in the bag. "That one's Frederick," he said. He called Chase Eddy's number, just in case, but the other agent's pocket began to buzz. Eddy reached into his pocket and hit a button to turn it off. Palmer ended the call and tried Alex McKenna's line.

The cell phone in the other bag lit up. "Interesting," he said.

"How would Lindy get Alex's phone?" Eddy asked.

"I don't know," Palmer said, eyeing him. "But I intend to find out."

Chapter 6

ORLAND PARK, ILLINOIS
SATURDAY MORNING

ORLAND PARK TURNED OUT to be one of many small
commuter villages that surrounded Chicago on all sides.
It wasn't nearly as rich and swanky as the northern
coastal suburbs, but it was a pretty average representa-
tion. Actually, Lindy thought as they climbed out of the
cab, it looked pretty average on all counts: size, facilities,
population, and so on. It was inconspicuous, which was
what you wanted in a rendezvous point—or a clandes-
tine meeting.

The weather was still overcast, and a cold wind had
picked up, which left the park nicely uninhabited for a
Sunday. They walked to a small, deserted pavilion with
two benches right across from each other and sat down
on one, both of them eyeing the surroundings on the
off chance they'd been followed. Lindy was wearing her
denim jacket, but she wished she'd worn pants, or at least
a longer dress. Being a shade didn't make you immune to

the cold—at least not during daylight hours.

Ruiz, who lived in Brookfield, arrived first, wearing beat-up jeans and a Leinenkugel's beer T-shirt. He grunted a greeting and plopped down on the bench opposite Alex and Lindy. He gave the bundle of brown paper between them a curious look, but seemed comfortable waiting for Hadley.

She appeared a few minutes later, also from the direction of the parking lot. Hadley was wearing the same black slacks and green blouse she'd had on the day before, although now the blouse was untucked. She had pulled up the front sides of her long red hair, leaving the rest of it hanging down to her waist, which helped soften the look. She looked a little flushed and embarrassed as she walked over, but her jaw was set stubbornly, practically daring them to comment. None of them did. She sat down on the edge of Ruiz's bench. "Hi," she said. "What the hell's going on?"

Alex told them everything: the hijacked van, the attack on BPI headquarters in Washington, Chase's missing time, the arrest warrant for Lindy. It seemed only fair, given the risks they would be taking just by associating with him and Lindy. The only thing he left out was his sleepover at Lindy's house, but his agents were no dummies. "How did you manage to get to Lindy before Gil's team?" was Hadley's first question.

"I was already with her," Alex said levelly.

"Oh." A beat, and then Hadley repeated, "Oh."

Lindy saw Alex cock an eyebrow at her, as if to say, "You really want to go there?" The younger agent pretended to be very interested in watching a passing cyclist. Ruiz glanced quickly back and forth between Alex and Lindy for a moment, then shrugged to himself. He didn't look comfortable, but he also didn't comment.

Instead, he asked, "So what's the plan?"

"The same as it's always been," Alex replied. "Catch Hector." He touched the bundle of papers. "Lindy's already gotten us a head start."

It was nice of him to not mention that Lindy had been holding out on all of them.

"But, boss," Hadley broke in, "you can't pretend that nothing's changed. Lindy's a federal fugitive, we're suspended, and you're AWOL, or you will be soon. And God knows what's gonna happen to Agent Eddy."

"All of which is exactly what Hector wants," Lindy reminded her.

"You really think it goes that deep?" Ruiz asked.

Lindy paused, considering the question. "I think Hector's been moving us around like game pieces, yeah. This team thwarted his plans, and I killed his pet psycho killer. He doesn't take that lightly. He wanted to break Ambrose out of jail and get Reagan on his side, and he wanted to embarrass and divide us. He used Chase to do all of it in two moves." She didn't bother to keep the bitterness out of her voice.

"So what's he expecting us to do now?" Hadley asked her.

Lindy nodded approvingly. It was the right question. "He's counting on breaking us up. Alex goes to Washington, I go into hiding, you two . . . I don't know, get transferred or go on leave. Either way, you're off the board. And he's arranged it so the only real alternative for any of us is to go to jail."

"The only *legal* alternative," Ruiz said, his expression very innocent.

Alex gave him and Hadley a hard look. "Let me make this clear. Lindy and I are going after Hector. If you help us, you could lose your jobs, or possibly even go to prison. Or, you know, Hector might kill us all. If, on the other hand, you want to report in, report *us*"—he pointed to Lindy and himself—"I really will understand. You don't owe me your whole career."

Hadley and Ruiz glanced at each other momentarily and then turned back to face Alex. "We're with you, boss," Hadley said quietly.

The gruff veteran agent nodded with intense determination. Ruiz had been with the Chicago BPI pod before any of them. He was the last surviving member of the original team, the one Hector killed entirely. "Let's get this fucker."

Alex's shoulders seemed to loosen a little in relief. Hadley asked, "But how do we start?"

Lindy smiled. "By being unpredictable. Hector doesn't think we're going to keep hunting him, and if we do, I can promise you he expects us to chase him to DC, divided and without the backing of the BPI."

"So we stay right here, in Chicago," Alex added.

Lindy nodded. "And we try to find out where he might be hiding."

"What do you need?" Ruiz asked.

"First of all, a place to work," Alex said. "By now the deputy director's office has realized I'm *not* on my way to Washington. They'll be watching my apartment and Lindy's brownstone, and I expect they'll be keeping an eye on your places as well."

They all fell silent for a minute, thinking it over. "A hotel room?" Lindy asked.

Alex shook his head. "Too many witnesses and video cameras. If the BPI puts us on the news, which seems likely, we'll be identified quick."

Lindy felt a rush of panic. Until now the whole day had seemed like kind of a lark, but now it was getting real.

"My cousin Sadie owns rental cabins not too far from here," Hadley offered. "They're nothing fancy—each one's just a big room with a couple of beds and a kitchenette—but they're pretty private."

"Would she let you use one?" Alex asked.

Hadley nodded. "I could just tell her my department has been suspended and I need to blow off some steam with a few friends."

"That's barely even a lie," Alex said, nodding. "Okay, you guys head there. Lindy and I need to make a stop first."

Chapter 7

FBI LABS
SATURDAY AFTERNOON

"**YOU CALLED ME IN** on a Saturday to get you *methamphetamines*?"

Alex thought Noelle Liang, the Chicago FBI's star engineer, looked more perplexed than outraged. They were in her office/lab space, a tennis court–sized room with a massive metal desk tucked into a back corner and rows of tables full of equipment Alex didn't recognize. Noelle was in charge of the Chicago Bureau's technology: recording, listening, and tracking devices, and now even smart weapons. If it had multiple working parts or needed to be plugged in, Noelle had either created it or maintained it, or both.

She could be making a fortune in the private sector, but Noelle obviously liked her work, and her brilliance allowed her to keep a fairly Monday–Friday schedule ... and get away with her own personal dress code. Today she was wearing big clunky motorcycle boots with torn jeans and a black tank top with a picture of a kitten wearing glasses. It was the weekend, but Alex had seen her wear more or less the same outfit on a Wednesday.

Getting in the building hadn't been as difficult as Alex had feared. Noelle's office was close to the building's rear entrance, so it didn't involve passing a bunch of witnesses, and Lindy had mesmerized two security guards and a janitor to forget they'd been there. The security guard had been perfectly content to erase the security footage of their arrival.

Noelle herself was the bigger risk: Alex didn't know her very well, but even he could see that despite her punk hairdo and cavalier attitude, she loved her job with the Bureau. She didn't seem alarmed or worried when they walked in. Even so, Lindy was leaning against a wall at least ten feet away, so Noelle wouldn't be worried about getting mesmerized. She had pulled down the sleeves of her denim jacket so Noelle wouldn't notice the missing bracelet.

"No," Alex said. "I can find some assholes and steal meth. I called you in on a Saturday to make me a dart gun that can deliver it quickly."

Noelle looked thoughtful. "I got the text bulletin about the two shade attacks on the Bureau this morning," she said. "And I have a friend who works for CNN in DC who says that there are a number of anti-shade protests going on in DC tonight and tomorrow. What am I missing, McKenna?"

Alex and Lindy exchanged a look. No one at the Bureau had told Noelle they suspected Lindy's involvement... which explained why she hadn't pulled the fire alarm the moment they'd walked in.

In his head, Alex heard Lindy's voice say, *If you tell her, she might sound the alarm.* It was scary how he was getting used to hearing her like that.

Alex gave a tiny head shake and said, "Look, Noelle, the truth is that the deputy director thinks Lindy was involved in the attacks. But I know she didn't do it. Lindy wants to get Hector even more than we do."

Noelle gave Lindy a wary look. "No offense, but why should I believe that? Couldn't you just have mesmerized Alex to bring you here and ask me for this?"

"That's a fair question," Lindy admitted. "But, look, do you know how shade saliva works?"

"The shade touches saliva to the victim's skin, which triggers hallucinogenic properties after absorption. This makes the recipient pliable and suggestible," Noelle replied, sounding like she'd memorized an official memo. Maybe she had.

"Yeah. Watch." Lindy stepped toward them, and Noelle immediately backed away toward the wall—but Lindy just touched her finger to her mouth and then laid her hand on Alex's arm. "Alex," she said in a low, hypnotic voice, "stand on one foot."

Alex shot her a grin. "Nah."

Noelle didn't look convinced. "How do I know you really got shade saliva on your finger?" she pointed out.

Damn. Alex should have known Noelle would react like a scientist. Before Lindy could answer, Alex reached for her waist and pulled her close. Lindy's eyes were startled—*really?*—but Alex dipped his head and kissed her, long enough to leave absolutely no uncertainty. When Lindy finally pulled back, Alex was a little breathless.

"Whoa," Noelle said under her breath. "Okay. I don't usually say this about straight people, but that was hot."

Alex raised his eyebrows at Lindy, who looked slightly flustered. Then she pulled herself together, looked around for a second, and said, "Alex, pick up that pencil."

Alex smiled at her and crossed his arms over his chest. He glanced at Noelle, whose eyes widened. Circling around Lindy, she picked up a penlight from the scattered supplies on the table and pulled on Alex's shoulder so he would turn toward her. He held still while she shone the light into his eyes. "Normal pupil response," she said, mostly to herself. "You're one of the immune."

A tiny percent of the population was naturally resistant to shade saliva—just as a tiny percent was particularly vulnerable to it. Noelle took a step back, studying the BPI agent.

"And I know for a fact that Lindy wasn't involved in either attack," Alex told her. "She was with me all night."

"Oh. *Oh*. Right." Noelle chewed on the inside of her cheek for a moment. "Lindy could have set it up in advance and used you for her alibi," she pointed out, but her voice lacked conviction.

"Without even a call or a text message to tell her the job was successful?" he countered, shaking his head. "Look, I trust her. My pod trusts her. And one thing I know for sure is that if Lindy is sent to Camp Vamp, we have no chance of catching Hector without a lot of lives lost."

Noelle studied him for a long moment, then nodded to herself. "All right," she said. "I never found out that Lindy is wanted for questioning. Why meth?"

As Lindy explained how the synthetic drug worked to short out a shade's nervous system, Noelle's eyes lit up. The Bureau had spent months searching for a weapon that worked better than "use a whole bunch of bullets" and she was obviously excited to finally have an answer.

"Okay," she said when Lindy finished. "As far as I'm concerned, Alex asked me to come in and work on this weapon in response to the attack on Camp Vamp. Got it?"

"Got it," they both said.

Everyone sat down, and Noelle took notes while Lindy described the dart gun that Reagan had used. The engineer asked a couple of follow-up questions about the speed and trigger mechanism, and then she turned to Alex. "This shouldn't be too hard. It's pretty simple to get the type of dart guns used at zoos and national parks, but given the reaction speed we've seen from shades, I'd likely want to boost the dart velocity and maybe the trigger response. I'll also need to figure out dosage requirements and make sure the—"

She broke off as her desk phone began to ring. They all looked at each other. "I didn't tell anyone I was coming in," she said before Alex could ask. Noelle went over and picked up the phone.

"Hello?" She listened for a moment, growing concerned. "Okay, thanks, Lionel."

She slammed the receiver down. "That was the security desk at the front of the building. Gil Palmer is on his way."

Chapter 8

WHEN NOELLE AGREED TO help them, Lindy almost sagged with relief. She was fairly weak at the moment, given the daylight and the time outside, and she'd already put a lot of effort into escaping Gil's team and mesmerizing the guards. She hadn't been looking forward to the effort of mesmerizing Noelle, too.

And then Gil himself arrived.

He was coming from the front of the building, but he'd have to use the same hallway they would need to exit. Lindy was preparing herself to attack and mesmerize him when Noelle made a shooing motion. "Just . . . go hide!"

That seemed kind of ridiculous, but before Lindy could say so, Alex darted toward the attached bathroom. He went in without turning on the light, leaving the door cracked open. Lindy shrugged to herself. It seemed silly, but hiding would be easier than mesmerizing Gil Palmer before he could get to his gun. She went to Noelle's desk and tucked herself into the footwell.

They heard the footsteps a moment later, and then Palmer's familiar voice. "Hey, kid."

"Hey," Noelle replied. "I'm twenty-seven, *old man*." But it was said affectionately, like they'd had the exchange many times before.

"Still a kid to me. What are you doing in today?"

"Just working on a pet project," Noelle said. "What's up?"

"I was wondering if you could get anything off these for me."

Lindy heard the sound of something plastic being laid on the table. "Cell phones?" Noelle sounded surprised. "Dude, we have technicians who specialize in these. I'm an engineer."

"I know, but this is delicate. You heard about the attacks on the detention facility, and the transportation van?"

"I did."

"We think Rosalind Frederick was involved. This phone here is hers, and the other is Alex McKenna's."

There was a brief pause, and then Noelle asked, "Where did you get these?"

"I found them at Frederick's house this morning. No sign of her or Alex."

"And what's your evidence against Lin—uh, Rosalind Frederick?" Noelle sounded genuinely curious, and Lindy suspected she didn't totally trust that Alex was telling the truth.

Gil made a scoffing sound. "Come on, Noelle. I know you're in on the fact that she's Hector's sister. And Hector's people magically escape custody, only weeks after Frederick signs on to help us? It's so obvious."

Lindy rolled her eyes. Gil had always struck her as a smart man, but he wasn't exactly a creative thinker.

Noelle must have agreed, because her next comment was, "That's circumstantial as hell, Gil."

"Yeah, well, that's why I need you to get into these phones. Going through the phone carriers will take forever, especially on a weekend, and we're trying to keep Lindy's involvement quiet internally until we can locate her. Can you do it?"

There was a long pause, with only the sound of plastic crinkling, as though Noelle were examining the phones through the bag. "I can try," she said at last.

"Thanks." Gil sounded relieved . . . but there were no immediate footsteps, or any other sign that he was leaving.

After an awkward pause, Noelle asked, "How is Lori doing these days?"

"She's . . ." Palmer sounded surprised, then dejected. "Not so great. The cancer is progressing faster than her doctors had hoped."

"Send her my best, okay?"

"Thanks. Thanks for asking about her, kid."

"You're welcome, *old man*."

At last, there were shuffling footsteps in the direction of the door, and Lindy started to relax. But then Palmer said, "Hey, you mind if I use your bathroom quick before I go?"

Lindy cursed inwardly, but Noelle didn't miss a beat. Her voice was perfectly casual as she said, "It's clogged, actually. Maintenance can't get to it until Monday. But there's one down the hall to the right."

Lindy waited to hear Palmer's footsteps, but they didn't come. There was a long, pregnant moment of silence, and then Palmer said in a studiously casual voice, "I'll just wash my hands then."

He began moving toward the bathroom, ignoring all of Noelle's further attempts at dissuading him. The bathroom was on the wall opposite the desk, so Lindy silently pushed the rolling chair away from her, coiling herself to spring across the room. She leaned her head far enough out to see Palmer, his back to her, reaching for the bathroom door.

And then she realized how Alex was going to react: violently. If he attacked Gil Palmer, even just to knock him out, this thing would snowball even further. Lindy had one second to decide.

Alex, stay right there.

She pushed the rolling chair hard, so it slammed backward into the wall with a *thunk* that could be heard over Noelle's protestations. Both she and Gil went quiet.

"What was that?" Palmer said.

"Uh . . . maybe one of the rats escaped from the lab down the hall?"

Lindy heard a quiet snap, and knew Palmer was pulling out his weapon. She raised her hands and slowly stood up. "I'm here, Agent Palmer. I was mesmerizing Noelle to help me."

As she'd expected, Palmer had the sidearm pointed at her chest. "Where is Alex McKenna?" he said, practically snarling.

Don't you dare come out, Alex. "On his way to Washington, as far as I know."

She was a good liar. Uncertainty flickered in his eyes, but only briefly. "How did you get his cell phone?"

Lindy feigned confusion. "What are you talking about?"

"It was found at your place this morning."

She shrugged. "He came in for coffee last night after he dropped me off. He must have forgotten it."

Gil seemed to decide that further questioning could wait. "I'm taking you into custody," he announced.

Lindy suddenly felt weary. The day had already been far too thrilling. Moving very slowly, she sat down in the chair, ignoring Palmer's shout of protest. "Really?" she said. "How do you plan to do that?"

Palmer eyed Noelle. "Kid, go get me some help."

"I mesmerized her, remember?" Lindy countered. "Stay right there, Noelle."

Noelle froze, a look of surprise and indecision on her face. They both knew Lindy hadn't touched her. If she obeyed Palmer, he would know that she hadn't really been mesmerized, which would mean she had voluntarily helped Lindy hide from him. Then again, if Noelle stayed still, she'd have to carry on the charade and do whatever Lindy told her. She stayed where she was, but shot Lindy a look that said, *I hope you know what you're doing.*

Palmer missed this because his eyes were locked on Lindy. His face was stony, but when she concentrated a moment she could hear his pulse racing. He was terrified of her. Smart.

"You know I could take that gun away from you, right?" she said mildly, leaning back in the chair. Palmer's lips tightened briefly, but he said nothing. "I'm not necessarily faster than a bullet, you understand, but I can certainly dodge out of the way in time, even during daylight hours. I can probably cross the room and take the gun away before you get another chance to aim." Lindy gave a little shrug, as if none of it made a difference to her. "Then I can mesmerize you to do whatever I want."

Palmer's pulse picked up even further, which made sense. He was enough of a control freak that the thought of being mesmerized scared him more than gunfire. "So how about we do this," Lindy suggested. "You sit down on the stool and let me explain a few things. If you still want to take me in after that, I'll go willingly. Promise."

His eyes narrowed. "How can I possibly trust your word on that? I don't know you, I don't know *what* you did with Alex McKenna, and—"

"I'm right here, Palmer."

Gil Palmer jumped, instinctively turning to point his weapon at the bathroom door as Alex came through it, looking sheepish. He held his hands away from his body so Gil could see he was unarmed.

Dammit, Alex! I had this under control.

"You're *with* her?" Gil said incredulously. He lowered the weapon, glancing back and forth between Lindy and Alex. "She's mesmerized you, man!"

"He's immune," Noelle said quietly. Gil's head snapped around as he took this in. "Trust me," Noelle added. "It's true."

Finally, he put the gun back in the holster, but kept his hand on it. "All right," he said to Lindy, "what the hell is going on?"

Chapter 9

CHICAGO'S LITTLE ITALY
SATURDAY MORNING

SLOANE DROVE THE MASSIVE Hummer past the abandoned building for a third time, his head craned to look for any signs of a trap. An impatient SUV driver behind him blared a horn, and Sloane winced, hoping it wouldn't wake Reagan. She needed the rest. She really wasn't old enough to stay awake more than a couple of hours at the beginning and end of the day.

He waved at the driver to go around and scrutinized the building where he and Reagan had holed up for a couple of weeks before the advance on Switch Creek. They hadn't actually intended to come back here, but nothing seemed to have changed. He wasn't even sure what the building had formerly been used for—storage? office space?—but it had a large basement with blacked-out windows that made a perfect bunker. Reagan and the others would have no reason to tell the police about this place, but he needed to be sure there wasn't a trap waiting for them.

Finally, Sloane parked the Hummer in the garbage-strewn alley behind the building, where it was hidden from the road. He went in alone through the broken back door, and found everything in the basement exactly as he and Reagan had left it. They had taken their camping equipment with them—he had no idea where it had ended up, probably in a police impound lot in Switch Creek—but the floors would have to do.

Sloane hauled in the two airtight body bags first, one at a time, because that's what Reagan would want him to do. When he hurried back for her he didn't have the heart to stuff her back in the body bag, so he just sort of draped it over her and carried her inside. She felt so light in his arms.

With that done, Sloane allowed himself to collapse on the cool concrete floor. He and Reagan had both fed off the guards at the accident scene—they were dead or nearly dead by then—but this was still a lot of daylight activity for him. He wanted to figure out their next move, but his eyes were already drifting shut. Sloane fought it for a few minutes, then gave up and stretched out next to Reagan.

Just a few hours of rest.

~

COZY CONIFER CABINS
LATE SATURDAY MORNING

The cabins were just as Hadley remembered.

She had many fond memories of running around the grounds with her cousins as a child, when her aunt Rose and uncle Julian had managed the cabins. Her cousin Sadie had inherited the property a few years ago, but she was a lackluster manager, putting very little effort into keeping the former family business afloat. Hadley was no longer close to Sadie, who had married young and had three kids with a guy Hadley suspected of at least a few white-collar crimes. Sadie didn't need the money from the cabins, and she had three young kids to take care of. The cabins were really only open at all out of her distracted sense of obligation.

All of which worked in Lindy's favor now. When she'd called her cousin, Sadie had readily agreed to let them have Bear Cub Cabin, the second-largest, and told Hadley where to find the key. The building was in bad need of a paint job, but it was secluded and quiet, with remarkably good wi-fi. That had been Sadie's one new contribution to the business: she'd figured she could attract businessmen and writers for retreats. Hadley had no idea if it worked, but the cabin was perfect for what they needed.

She and Ruiz had stopped at a Target for clothes and supplies, then unfolded, smoothed, and hung all of the brown paper along two walls of the cabin. They had to move some of the furniture around and paper over a closet door, but in the end, as they stepped back to look at it, Hadley could immediately see how the whole exercise was worth it. She reached up and touched a thick black line that seemed to serve as a partial timeline of Hector's life. "You see the starting date on this?"

Ruiz glanced where she was looking. "Yeah." He sounded a little unnerved. The first mark on the timeline was labeled "turned into a shade," and the year listed was 721.

Lindy was more than thirteen hundred years old.

"I'm trying not to think about it too much," Ruiz admitted.

"Seems reasonable."

They surveyed the paper for another minute, and then Ruiz shook his head, looking a little disgusted. "She's been keeping a hell of a lot from us, you know."

"I know."

"But you still trust her?"

Hadley took a moment to consider it. Only a couple of days before, the answer would have been no. But she was vigilant about making sure Lindy didn't touch her, didn't go near anything Hadley ate or drank. She didn't think the shade had ever mesmerized her—and Lindy had put her life on the line more than once for the BPI pod. If she was playing them, Hadley couldn't see how.

So why keep all this Hector background from them? "She was protecting us," Hadley concluded. "And maybe protecting our image of her."

"What does that mean?"

Hadley pointed at the notations again. "Look, there's a lot of detail right at the beginning of this, and starting about halfway across, all the entries are a few years apart. Like she was keeping tabs on him, but from a distance."

Ruiz stared at the first half of the timeline and nodded. "You think they were together at first?"

"Yeah." Hadley touched an entry that read, "killed the mayor of Warsaw." The date listed was 1849. "And Lindy might not have been helping him, but she didn't stop him, either."

"Maybe that's how we got here," Ruiz grumbled. "I agree that Lindy is with us—now—but a hell of a lot of pain could have been avoided if she'd just killed her brother a couple hundred years ago."

Hadley looked at him. "You got any siblings?"

"A brother. Four years younger."

"Is he smart? Successful?"

Ruiz snorted. "Nah. He works part-time as a grounds-keeper at Wrigley."

"And if you found out that he killed someone, would you turn him in?"

Ruiz's head snapped toward her, his eyes narrowing. Then he shrugged and looked away. "Point taken."

There was an awkward pause, and then the older BPI agent crossed the room to the other end of the timeline. "Anyway. Thirteen hundred years of history is too much to sift through."

"Overwhelming," Hadley agreed.

"But if Hector were just any other guy, we'd be looking for known associates and previous residences. So we should start over here."

Hadley followed him. The last entry on the timeline was from just the night before: "Called to brag about corrupting Reagan."

"Okay, so let's work backward," she said. Before the phone call, there were notes from Hector's experiments on transmuting teenagers over the summer. Before that, the most recent entry was for 2002. Before *that*, the entries were pretty evenly spaced, every two or three years apart.

So why the long gap between 2002 and the summer?

"Lindy told us once that she and Hector can feel each other's location, right?" Hadley said, thinking out loud. "But Lindy gets a total blood transfusion to keep him out of her head."

"Right . . ."

"That can't be as simple as hooking up a couple of needles," Hadley reasoned. "She'd need equipment, a lot of blood, and most of all, someone she really trusts. She'll be vulnerable as hell when she's basically drained of blood."

"Where are you going with this?"

"Well, we can confirm it with Lindy, but let's say 2002 is when she gets the first transfusion. Before that, they were in each others' business every couple of years. Probably couldn't help it."

"Or one of them was chasing the other," he pointed out.

"True," she acknowledged. Hadley studied the timeline a moment longer, tapping an index finger on her lower lip. Then she dug the burner phone out of her pocket.

"Who are you calling?"

"Lindy." Hadley found the number for Alex's new burner and hit the number. As she waited for it to connect, she explained, "If she has to keep having these transfusions, that means they wear off, right?"

"Right . . ."

"Hector can't know when Lindy's transfusion will wear off, and right now, he doesn't want *her* to be able to find *him*. So what if whoever she uses to do the transfusion is someone Hector knows too?"

Chapter 10

ALEX COULDN'T TELL HOW Gil was reacting to Lindy's explanation—the FBI agent had a pretty good poker face. He did look a little skeptical, though.

"You think Hector's setting you up on purpose?" Gil said. "He put all these moving parts in play so you'd be, what, ostracized by the Bureau?"

"I think that me signing on with the BPI surprised him, and he did everything he could do to undo it," she replied. "But he's going to have a bigger plan in play, and the best way to oppose him is to keep surprising him."

"But how did he know about Camp Vamp?" Gil insisted. "There's no way he could have broken in and freed the prisoners without insider knowledge."

Lindy looked at Alex, and he heard her voice in his head again. *Up to you.*

Alex took a deep breath. "One of my team members revealed the information under duress," he told Gil.

"Hector mesmerized this individual. It was not his or her fault."

Gil rolled his eyes. "It's Chase Eddy, isn't it?"

Alex was ready for the question, and made sure his face didn't so much as twitch. "I'm not going to say which of my team members was involved. But if you happen to still have Agent Eddy in custody, I would remind you that you have no evidence of any wrongdoing on his part."

Gil looked ready to call bullshit on that, but Lindy broke in before he could respond, "Look, Gil. Let's say for a second that you and the rest of the BPI are right about me, and I'm totally in cahoots with my evil twin brother. Hector has already gotten his people out of Camp Vamp, and killed even more BPI officers, including"—her voice wobbled for just a moment, but pushed on—"Agent Bartell, who has been with the BPI since the beginning. Why exactly would I be hanging around now? Why wouldn't I kill you and Alex and run off to join Hector for our next evil scheme?"

That seemed to give Gil pause, although Alex wasn't sure if it was because she made a good point or because she'd used the phrase "evil twin brother."

"Here's the bottom line, man," Alex said, drawing Gil's attention again. "You saw Lindy fight with us that night at the clinic." The memory seemed to make Gil twitch a little. "Hector is as old as she is, as strong as she is. Do you want to go up against him? Or can we send in our heavy-weight?"

Gil looked back and forth between them, then glanced at Noelle. She held her hands up. "I just make the toys," she said. "But for what it's worth, I believe them. And she's right, if all she wanted to do was help Hector, there's no reason for her to stick around now."

Gil sighed, dry-scrubbing his face with both hands. "All right," he said. "Here's what we'll do: I'll give you two forty-eight hours to get this asshole. But Lindy puts the bracelet back on." He reached into his pocket and held up the tracer bracelet that Noelle had designed. It was still in a plastic evidence bag.

Lindy looked ready to agree, but Alex couldn't help but say, "How do we know you won't just use the bracelet to hunt us down when you've got your team behind you?"

Gil gave him a look. "Call it a leap of faith."

He had to admit, this was fair. And it occurred to him that if he and Lindy did find Hector, it might not be a bad idea for Gil and the cavalry to be able to find them.

After that, things moved quickly. Noelle entered a new code into the bracelet, and this time she gave it to Gil, not Alex. Gil made a show of checking his watch. "Forty-eight hours, then I'm coming to get you, Hector or not," he warned. "And I'm hanging around Noelle until then.

Making sure you don't try to get the code from her."

Noelle made a face. Alex asked her, "Can you still make the weapons?"

Gil looked between them. "Wait, what weapons?"

"Yeah," Noelle answered, brightening a little. To Gil, she said, "You can be my lab assistant."

The older agent blanched, but before he could respond, Lindy stood up. "We should get going," she said. Then she paused and gave Alex a rueful look. *I don't suppose the El goes all the way to Hadley's cabin?*

Noelle looked back and forth between them for a second and said, "Wait." She went over to the backpack on her desk and dug out a set of keys, removing a single key fob and tossing it to Alex. "It's the red Prius in the back lot. I can ride my Harley until you get it back to me."

He nodded. "Thanks, Noelle."

They headed for the door, but Lindy paused. She turned and said over her shoulder, "Oh, and Gil? While we're finding my brother, could you be a lamb and get us some methamphetamine?"

Noelle had actual CDs all over the Prius's passenger seat, but Alex scooped them up and deposited them in the back seat, along with some takeout wrappers and several empty water bottles. While he cleared the seats, Lindy leaned against the car frame looking tired and wan. Before they'd left, Noelle had requested a blood sample so she could use it in developing dosages for the darts. Alex had worried that Lindy didn't have the extra blood to lose, but he'd said nothing. It wasn't his place, and besides, it was a show of faith in Noelle that Lindy trusted her with her blood. The last person who'd asked her for a sample was Hector.

"So," Alex said as they finally climbed into the car. "'Be a lamb'? Were you *trying* to piss off Palmer?"

Despite her obvious fatigue, Lindy grinned at him. "Come on, you don't want to waste our time beating up drug dealers in redneck bars in Wisconsin. That's a Palmer job."

"Beating up redneck drug dealers sounds a lot more fun than going after Hector," he grumbled.

The new burner phone had internet and GPS, so Lindy navigated and Alex drove them toward Hadley's cousin's cabin. After about twenty minutes, the phone rang in Lindy's hand. "Probably Hadley and Ruiz," Alex guessed.

"Hello?" she said cautiously, then Alex could see her relax. "Oh, hey, Hadley." She listened for a second, and her face clouded over with worry. "Shit," she whispered. "Okay. No, it's a good point. I'll make a call."

"What's up?" Alex asked as soon as she hung up.

"Can you stop for a minute?" He pulled the car over, and she entered another number into the phone, and waited while it rang. And rang. Lindy tried two more times, and then turned to Alex. "We need to make a detour," she said shortly.

"To where?"

"Aurora. I need to check on a friend."

Chapter 11

"SO HOW IS IT that this friend you've had for hundreds of years just happens to live forty miles west of us?" Alex said around a mouthful of sub sandwich. They'd made a quick stop so he could grab lunch.

"I *asked* Roza to move closer to me," Lindy explained. "She arrived from New York a couple of weeks ago."

"You must be close, if she came all the way to Chicago to be near you."

"Yes and no. Roza was the great-granddaughter of our nursemaid, Hilda," Lindy told him.

Whoa. That would make her almost as old as Lindy. "How does that work?"

"Hector and I loved Hilda. After she died, we kept an eye on her descendants. Roza was the last one, and she contracted a fatal illness when she was about forty."

"So you transmuted her?"

Lindy shook her head. "Hector and I were both in

Prague, and worried that we wouldn't make it back in time. But we sent an emissary to do it."

"So now you're . . . friends?"

Lindy smiled faintly. "Of a sort. Roza is like that cousin you don't always get along with, but you're still family. She's also brilliant. She developed the technique that keeps Hector from finding me."

Alex rode along in silence for a few minutes, unsure of how much to question Lindy. She usually only talked about her past in a vague way, like she was just too used to keeping secrets to even consider opening up. But then again, he'd never invited her to.

"How were *you* transmuted?" he asked tentatively.

Lindy looked out the Prius's window. "It's a long story."

"It'll be almost another hour to Aurora," Alex offered. "And I don't know about you, but I didn't recognize *any* of Noelle's music."

Lindy smiled again, and he reached over and squeezed her hand. "You don't have to tell me about it," he said. "But it might help me understand."

She nodded. "All right." Her eyes grew distant for a moment, as if looking for a starting place. "In 541, the first outbreak of the bubonic plague spread across the Roman Empire. Shades must have existed by then, but in very few numbers, which is partly why it was able to spread so quickly—there were no shades to boost the humans' immunity." She shook her head. "I wasn't alive yet, but historians today believe that something like thirteen percent of the world's population died, Alex. For a time it really did seem like the end of the world. So the shades, who were immune, of course, began to organize themselves."

"Organize how?"

"They infected as many people as possible," she said flatly. "They treated the shade strain almost as a vaccine against the plague." She paused, considering. "No, more than that. It wasn't just that every new shade was immune to the plague. They also fed off humans who desperately needed the increased immunity to fight off the infection. Emperor Justinian contracted the plague and survived, supposedly because he had his own personal shade feeding off him at the time."

"Jesus." Alex tried to imagine what it must have been like: competing infections racing across Europe, each one destroying humanity as it was understood then. Becoming a shade must have seemed like the lesser evil.

As soon as he thought that, he felt a little guilty. Lindy wasn't an evil, lesser or otherwise.

She must have read the thoughts on his face, because she just gave him a grim smile and continued the story. "I have no idea how many shades existed before the Plague of Justinian, as the history books now call it, but that was the first shade outbreak, the first controlled effort to balance the shade-human proportions more favorably."

"Did it work?" Alex asked. "Did it stop the plague?"

"Slowed it down enough for it to stop, yes," she said. "Although most humans weren't told about us. At the time, I believe shades were worried that too many humans would beg to become like them, and there would be no humans left to feed from." She rolled her eyes. "Ironic, right? They did learn something rather interesting about our kind, though: if you get enough brand-new shades together, there's a sort of herd mentality that takes hold."

"Big whoop," Alex scoffed. "Humans have that too."

She laughed. "I suppose they do. But I'm not talking about a psychological commonality. I mean more of a hive mind. Usually, shades have free will: an elder can *talk* to her fledglings, but she can't force them to do something. In a herd, though, they just sort of stop thinking. They listen to their creator and no other."

"That's what Hector was trying to do with the kids in Heavenly, wasn't he?" Alex said with sudden insight. "He wanted to replicate that."

"I suspect so," she replied. "He was hoping to connect a lot of shade minds at once, sort of like . . ." She frowned, thinking for a moment. "Like a power strip connected to many different strands of Christmas lights. Hector wanted to be the power strip."

Alex felt like there was probably a lap dance joke in there somewhere, but they'd strayed off topic. And he really wanted to know how Lindy had become a shade. "So there was this big vampire recruitment push . . ." he coaxed.

She chuckled. "Not how I'd phrase it, but okay. Anyway, after that, for the first time shades required their own leadership."

"How did they choose the leader?"

She pointed a finger at him. "Great question. During Late Antiquity, the western Roman Empire was divided into what are now called barbarian kingdoms, each with its own king," she said. "Think of them like the predecessor to the feudal system you learned about in high school. Barbarian kings inherited their throne, but the people also needed to consent to their leadership."

"Wait, what? How does that work?"

"Each king would have as many sons as possible, and his people would choose the one most worthy of ruling." She gave a wan smile. "Sometimes there was even a tie, and two kings ruled together as brothers."

"Okay . . ."

"So when all those new shades cast about for the oldest among them, they found a man named Rainer who had been turned twenty years *before* the bubonic plague began. And, funny thing, he was a barbarian . . . prince, I suppose you would say. Rainer's father was a Germanic king—of the Visigothic Kingdom, not that it matters much now—but the people had chosen his older brother to lead.

"Anyway, Rainer had married and had his own children and grandchildren before becoming a shade at the age of about fifty. He had twenty years' more experience as a shade than the generation around him, he was from a royal family, and it just made sense for him to become their king."

"So where do you come into the equation?" Alex asked, trying not to sound impatient.

"Aside from protecting the interests of shades, Rainer's biggest priority was protecting his family line. Shades can theoretically live forever, but he knew that eventually he would be killed, or the shade population would require additional leadership. At the very least, he'd wish to retire. So he kept his family line safe, and every few generations, he turned one or two of his descendants. Dynasties were very important back then, and he was creating a small cabinet of family members with absolute loyalty, you see?"

Alex nodded. "I met him once," she said, her face warming at the memory, "when I was a child. He was very kind to me. He seemed impossibly strong and capable—but there was a terrible weight to him. You know how the people who become president seem to age at a faster rate, due to the pressures of the office? Imagine having that pressure for two hundred years. Rainer was practically bowed over by it.

"Anyway." Her face clouded over. "Although King Rainer's line flourished, the Visigothic Kingdom began to die, as invading Arabs carved it away an inch at a time. The last Visigoth king, Ardo, begged King Rainer to rally the shades behind the Visigoths, but Rainer's primary loyalties were no longer with the humans. His concerns extended to thousands and thousands of shades who could live forever. He was heartsick for the end of the Visigoths, but he made the decision not to come to Ardo's aid."

She took a deep breath, and hugged her arms about herself. "So in revenge, Ardo gathered the last of his forces, and he sent them after Rainer's line. Which included me and my brothers and sisters."

Chapter 12

LINDY'S EYES WERE FAR AWAY, lost in an old horror. "But you and Hector survived?" Alex said, more to bring her back to the story than anything else.

She nodded. "Ardo's men attacked in the middle of the day, when Hector and I were out riding our horses. We were nineteen, and everything was a competition between us. While we were gone Ardo's men slaughtered everyone in the castle, including my mother, my little sisters, and my baby brother.

"My father was a new shade then, only transmuted a few weeks earlier. They dragged him out into the sunshine and left him to die." She shook her head. "He shouldn't even have been able to stay conscious during the day, but he managed to crawl into the stables, out of the sunlight. He was strong." She looked away for a moment, blinking, and Alex made himself wait for her. "Hector and I were racing back from the forest. I won, and I was laughing as I jumped down and led the horse into the stable. Then I saw Papa . . ." Her voice caught.

"And your father transmuted you," Alex supplied. He knew that the method of turning humans into shades had been risky and traumatic before modern medical equipment. He didn't need to make her relive that.

Lindy nodded, looking a little grateful. "And then Hector, right afterward. Papa died changing us into shades."

"Was that what you wanted?"

Lindy looked genuinely surprised at the question. "I . . ." She straightened up in her seat and pushed the hair behind her ears. "I did. When we were children, Hector was"—a tiny smile crossed her face—"the thinker. I was the better fighter, better fencer, better rider, but Hector was the superior strategist."

"So he was the brain, and you were the muscle," Alex said without thinking.

"I suppose so." Any good humor faded from her face as the meaning sunk in for her. "Anyway. Hector never wanted to be a shade, at least not then. It would have been our little brother, probably, or one of my sons, if I'd had any. But I longed to become immortal. I saw myself fighting alongside my great-great-great-grandfather and all his men, galloping around the continent to solve the problems of our people. Only it was never a possibility for women then. Rainer only made male soldiers."

Alex took her hand, lacing his fingers through hers. "It's all right," he said softly. "Just because you got your wish doesn't mean you're glad it happened that way."

She smiled at him, but she was still blinking away tears.

"Why did Hector agree to become a shade?" Alex asked.

"To avenge our family," she said simply. "If he had been first into the barn, Father would have turned him and left me to carry on the family line. But I arrived first, and by the time Father realized Hector had *also* survived, the process was already begun for me." She rolled her eyes. "And of course, he couldn't *not* transmute his last surviving male heir."

"So you're the last of your line," Alex concluded. "And you really are the queen of vampires."

"Oh, please." Lindy dabbed at her nose with her sleeve, a very human gesture. "The oldest among us still see it that way, and the younger generations—well, most of them are like that girl Reagan. They yearn for any leadership. But I always thought the shade monarchy, whatever there was of it, died with Rainer."

"Did Ardo's men kill him, too?"

"Yes. It took twelve of his best guards, though," she added, looking a little proud. "In broad daylight." She shook her head a little. "I can't believe I'm older now than he ever got to be. It's such a strange thought."

"What did you and Hector do after that?"

"We ran away together." She smiled. "That sounds like the beginning of a children's story, doesn't it, as though we joined the circus or something. But we were scared, and neither of us knew who we could trust. And we were brand-new shades. By the time we adjusted to our abilities and returned for revenge, Ardo had long since been killed in a different war." She shrugged. "So we traveled around. Hector studied science and math, and I learned languages, which was more appropriate for a woman. But we always kept an eye on Hilda's children and grandchildren—not just Roza. If any of them had a bad harvest, a financial gift would appear on their doorstep. That kind of thing." She looked out the window. "For a long time, we were content with that life. Then Hector began to have . . . ambitions."

"He wanted to be king," Alex guessed.

"More like he believed he *was* king," she corrected. "As Rainer's last male heir, he saw himself as a tragically exiled monarch, and he wanted to return to his throne."

"What about you?"

"I thought it was bullshit."

Alex chuckled. "Is that when you two parted ways?"

"More or less. For a long time, I think we both tried not to recognize that we were growing apart. Looking back, I was pretending not to see what Hector was, what he was becoming. At some point, he had stopped seeing humans as anything more than useful and occasionally entertaining cattle." She rolled her eyes. "And then that *damned* Abraham Stoker heard some vague rumors and published *Dracula,* and my brother became downright insufferable. He started to believe in the vampire legends, and began obsessing over the humans' reproduction rates and their effect on the planet.

"I tried to break away, but he was always finding me, urging me to rule with him. I don't think he really wanted that—he didn't want to *share* power. But he wanted me to see him ruling. By then, mine was the only opinion that mattered to him. Once in a while he would get aggressive about it, and I would remind him who was the better fighter."

Alex chuckled. "I can totally see that."

"Then Roza figured out how to shield me from him, and it was like being released from a tether. I owe her a lot."

"Did Hector at least leave you alone after that?"

Her faced darkened. "No. As more women became world leaders, Hector must have realized that my claim to the so-called vampire throne was equal to his own. It didn't matter whether or not I wanted it. He couldn't find me, so he began focusing on making sure I stayed as isolated as possible."

Alex remembered something she'd said at the Switch

Creek police station. Had that really been only the day before? "He killed your fledglings."

She nodded. "I never had many, but now and then I would grow close to a human and transmute them. The last one was in New York, thirty-four years ago. Rhys." Alex had seen that distant expression on the faces of many FBI agents, including his mother. Lindy was seeing him die again.

"You cared for him," he stated.

It seemed to snap Lindy out of her reverie. She drew a great, shuddering breath, and turned to Alex. "I loved him," she said simply. "And that was all Hector needed to decide Rhys had to die."

Alex understood now why she'd been so hesitant to get the pod involved with Hector. And why Bartell's death had hurt her so much. "Don't take this the wrong way," Alex said, hoping to lighten the mood, "but your brother sounds nuts."

She didn't laugh. "You're not wrong. He's spent hundreds of years thinking I stole his birthright, because I beat him in a horse race when we were nineteen. But being crazy isn't the same as being harmless."

The rest of the drive was quiet.

Chapter 13

APARTMENT JUST OUTSIDE AURORA, ILLINOIS
SATURDAY AFTERNOON

ROZA LIVED IN A basement apartment in a surprisingly large and modern building. Alex watched as Lindy pulled her foldable hat and sunglasses out of her purse and put them on, peering at the road in front of the structure. There weren't any cars parked on the road, but that didn't mean much.

"What are the odds that Hector's in there waiting for us?" he asked her.

She shook her head. "Slim to none. He would have attacked Camp Vamp in person, I'm sure of it. He would have wanted them to know he could." She checked her watch. "That was six hours ago, so I suppose there's a tiny chance he got right on a plane and got back here, but I truly doubt it."

Alex nodded, but he still checked his weapon, making sure there was a round in the chamber. It wasn't going to do much against Hector, but it could hopefully slow him down or surprise him enough for Lindy to attack. "Do you have your blades?" he asked.

She raised an eyebrow at him. "Stupid question," he acknowledged. Lindy had a special back harness for her twin push daggers, and her sundress was more than loose enough to hide it. "Let's go."

~

Lindy knocked and rang the bell, but when there was no answer she took a firm grip on the doorknob and started to twist hard, preparing to break the jamb. Instead, the knob turned easily in her hand.

That was when Alex suspected Roza was dead. From the grim look on Lindy's face, she did too.

They stepped inside, and the smell of old blood hit Alex's nostrils. It was everywhere: splashed on the cream carpeting and walls, dried along the lamps and framed art, congealing in a puddle on the coffee table. It looked like someone had set off a paint grenade filled with blood.

"She fought him," Lindy said softly. She crouched down near a particularly large puddle, and as Alex stepped sideways he could see that it was vaguely human-shaped. "But she died. Here."

Alex glanced around, noticing a security camera in the

corner, and another pointing at the hallway. "Where's the body?"

Lindy stood up. "He would have taken it. Even Hector wouldn't leave a shade body around to be dissected."

Alex looked carefully at the bloodstain on the lamp. "I've been to a lot of crime scenes," he said. "This happened a while ago. A week, maybe?"

"Closer to ten days."

"How do you know?" he asked, again without thinking.

Because that's what the blood is telling me, she answered in his head.

Right.

"There are security cameras," he pointed out. "There's footage of this somewhere."

She shook her head. "I would bet every penny in my considerable portfolio that he took it along. Come on."

Alex followed Lindy down the short hallway to a large back bedroom, which had been converted into a sort of clinic room, with a hospital bed, IV stands, a wastebasket, and several tables of equipment. A cheap disposable phone sat in the middle of the bed, but Lindy ignored it and went to look inside the wastebasket.

Just then, the phone let out an old-fashioned, pealing ring that made Alex jump. The screen said "BLOCKED NUMBER." "It's him," Lindy said with dull certainty.

Alex would love to trace the call, but how? Palmer might have given him a pass, but that didn't mean Alex had actual resources at his disposal right now.

Before he could decide, Lindy answered the phone on speaker.

"You didn't have to kill her," she said by way of hello.

Hector didn't miss a beat. "No, I didn't," he said smoothly. "But I had no reason not to, either."

Now Lindy looked angry. "You petulant *child*," Lindy said, her voice like a hiss of pressurized air. "She did nothing to you."

"That's where you're wrong," Hector replied. "She performed the same treatment on me that she has on you—with some of my people watching over her, of course. So you get what you want, Sieglinde. I'm out of your head. At least . . . in a literal sense." He chuckled. "Am I getting to you, sister?"

"Where are you?" Lindy demanded. She turned around in the room, as though he might somehow be hiding in a corner. "Still in Washington?"

"Now, why would I tell you that?"

"Because isn't that what you want?" she retorted. "You can't win the game if I don't show up to play."

"I've already won," he snapped. "You see what the humans are doing today? They're protesting us in the streets, Sieglinde. They are finally awake. And finally *afraid*."

"So, what, now you step forward and claim responsibility? They'll throw you right back into Camp Vamp."

"Responsibility? For what?" Hector sounded injured. "Aside from the consumption of human blood, which I admit to, I've committed no crimes."

"Bullshit." Her voice had risen.

"Oh, Lindy," Hector said in a pitying tone. "Don't get hysterical. I'm calling to make a deal."

"What deal?"

"Run away." His voice was light now, soothing. "Run away from Chicago, from your little BPI friends. You can try to find me, if that's really what you want, or you can disappear again. Off to play with your languages and your kitty cat."

Lindy didn't immediately respond, so Hector pushed on, sounding a little annoyed. "If you leave Chicago, I promise you, I won't come there. I won't kill Alex McKenna, Jill Hadley, Gabriel Ruiz, and my little buddy Chase. You've already destroyed their careers, little sister. Why not leave them their lives? Especially yours, Agent McKenna," he added.

Alex turned around and saw the camera above the doorway. Lindy followed his gaze, and her scowl deepened.

"Don't grind your teeth, Sieglinde," Hector said. "Good to see you again, Alex. That scar is really healing nicely."

Alex smiled at the camera and then raised his middle finger. *Don't antagonize him,* Lindy thought at him, but she was practically radiating anger.

"Has she slept with you yet, Alex?" Hector asked conversationally.

Alex tried to keep his face neutral, but he must have given something away. Hector laughed. "Oh, good for you! My sister can be a bit of a slut. I'm so happy you got to enjoy the spoils before you die."

Alex was about to respond—something childish—but Lindy picked up the cell phone first. Alex expected her to yell, but instead she said in a remarkably dry voice, "Hey, Hector? You're boring."

She hung up the phone, and Alex followed her out of the room.

~

When they were back in Noelle's Prius, Alex just sat for a minute without starting it. "That will piss him off, right?"

She smiled. "Oh, yeah. Hector does *not* like people hanging up on him."

"Good." He eyed her for a moment. "You're not going to run, are you?"

"I'm tempted," she admitted. "Not to hide, but to go face him head-on."

"It's not just that, though, is it? You want to keep us—the pod—out of it."

"Yes." She looked away, out her window. "What's left of you."

"Bartell wasn't your fault," Alex insisted. "And what happened to not playing into Hector's hand?"

She sighed. "I know." She leaned her head against the seat so she could look at him. "Let me ask you something," she said. "Say we do get Hector. I'd prefer to have him sent to Camp Vamp, but I accept that we may need to kill him. After that, though . . . what happens then?"

"Do you mean, like . . . us?"

She rolled her eyes. "That's not what I mean. Yes, I'm curious about our relationship, if we still have one—"

"If we still have one?" he echoed. "Why wouldn't we?"

"Because you"—she lifted a hand to touch his cheek—"are a federal agent. And I am currently a federal fugitive. We're like a bad prime-time drama."

"If it's any consolation," he offered, "I'm pretty sure I'm going to be fired."

She shook her head. "You'll get your job back. Or they'll put you in the mail room at the FBI, and you'll work your way back." She hesitated for a second, then added, "I read the 'Legacy Agent' article."

"Before or after you slept with me?" he said instantly. He was *mostly* kidding.

She laughed. "What I mean is, they'll take you back. It's who you are. But where does that leave me? How do you see this going?"

"I don't know," he said honestly. "I wish I did. But I really like you."

She made a gentle scoffing sound. "Okay, fine," Alex said, grinning. "That came out a *little* high school."

"A little?" Lindy smiled back, but she still looked troubled. He lifted her hand and kissed her knuckles.

"What is it?" he asked.

"Hector. He's always been better at strategy than me. Our father used to say that Hector thinks in layers. I don't know how to *find* him, much less how to beat him. And we're running out of time."

"I think if we can figure out the right draw, we might be able to get Hector to come to us," Alex said. "But is that really what's bothering you?"

"No," she admitted. "I just . . . I haven't done this before, having humans in my life. I kept a distance for a reason. What if he kills you or Hadley or Chase or Ruiz? What if he decides to come at me sideways, and goes after, I don't know, my mailman or Noelle or—"

"I have a feeling Palmer's not going to let Noelle out of his sight until our forty-eight hours are up," Alex interrupted. "And I'm pretty sure we're supposed to call them mail carriers now."

She swatted his arm, repositioning herself to face out the windshield. "You know what I mean."

"I know. But that's why we're going to meet up with the others and work the case," Alex said, trying to sound confident. "If we really can't find him, I will personally help you un-weld that bracelet, and you can run. Okay?"

She didn't look very reassured, but she nodded.

"Lindy," he said softly, and she looked over at him again. "Don't give up on me."

She blinked hard for a moment, then she laid her hand on his cheek. "Okay."

Alex pushed the button to start the Prius, glancing at the console clock as it came on.

"To the cabin?" Lindy asked.

"One more stop first."

"Where to?"

He shot her a lopsided smile. "The White House."

Chapter 14

ABANDONED BASEMENT IN LITTLE ITALY
SATURDAY AFTERNOON

"SLOANE."

Someone was touching his face. Sloane opened his eyes to see Reagan, her dark hair falling in her face. She smiled when she saw him open his eyes. "Hello," she said.

"What time is it?"

She lifted his forearm and read the watch on his wrist. "About three p.m."

Three hours until sunset. "You should get more rest, love."

"I'm okay." She did look much better than she had that morning, thanks to the cop's blood that he had fed her before putting her in the Hummer. Her hair still hung in matted clumps, but her eyes weren't so sunken now. "Thank you for saving us," she said seriously.

Sloane didn't say that he almost hadn't bothered with Cooper and Aidan. He had retrieved them because she would have been unhappy if he hadn't. "You're welcome."

Reagan sat up, putting her back against the wall. "God, I want a shower."

He smiled. "Can't blame you there, love." There weren't any showers in this building, just an old bathroom with a rust-stained sink. But at least there was running water.

They sat in silence for a few minutes, then he couldn't help but ask the question that had been plaguing him. "Why didn't you tell me you were taking orders from Hector?"

She puffed out her cheeks, released them. "You told so many stories about him, about the old days," she said. "I realize now that you were trying to warn me, but he always just sounded... powerful. In control." She gave a little head shake. "Shades need leadership, Sloane. I guess I told myself you were exaggerating his... bad qualities."

Sloane snorted.

"I know," she hurried to add. "I was stupid. But I just... worry. And I really did think Hector was trying to help."

And that's why I love you, he thought, but didn't say aloud. Sloane had never met another shade who cared so much about the well-being of all shades—well, except perhaps Hector, in his own twisted way. It didn't seem possible to be selfish and community-minded at the same time, but Hector was the proof.

"I feel so stupid now," Reagan admitted. "He was just using me, as part of his little sibling rivalry mind game. I'm such an idiot."

Sloane couldn't really blame Reagan for gravitating toward the eldest among them, but still. Reagan had told him they were coming to Chicago to look for information on her birth mother. She had lied to him. "Why didn't you just tell me you wanted to go work for him?" he asked. "I mean, I would have found out eventually, if things hadn't gone pear-shaped with Sieglinde."

Reagan hung her head. "Yeah, but you would have tried to talk me out of it. Besides," she added, "he told me over and over not to say anything."

Something about her phrasing raised a red flag in Sloane's head. He had spent so much time with Reagan, helping her mentor new shades, get them on their feet. He was with her most of her waking hours.

So . . . when would Hector have talked to her?

"He called you? On the phone?"

She turned her head and gave him a strange look. "No. He talked to me. In my head."

Sloane froze. *Oh no.* Very carefully, he said, "Rags . . . how did he say he was able to do that?"

"Because they're royalty," she said, as if she didn't understand why Sloane was pretending to be ignorant. "Hector and Sieglinde can speak to all shades. They just choose not to, because it'd be too taxing."

Sloane's heart wrenched. He forgot sometimes how young she was, and how she'd spent so many of her years with little to no contact with their kind. Reagan had woken up as a shade with no memory of how it happened, or who had attacked and transmuted her. And most of the shades Reagan met were like her, lost and abandoned.

"Reagan, love. No they can't." He kept his voice as gentle as he could, knowing how much this was going to hurt her. "I'm so sorry, I thought you knew. The only person who can speak in our mind is the one who transmuted us."

She pulled away, searching his face. "What did you just say?"

"Only our direct elder can speak to us through that link," he tried to explain. "My elder, Regina, used to give me orders and directions that way, before she died. It's part of how we're supposed to adapt to shade life. So if Hector could speak to you mentally . . ." He trailed off.

"It was him," she said, her voice barely a whisper. "He was the one. Why would he . . ."

"He must have been watching you, since you were human," Sloane guessed. "He saw something in you, and figured you'd be a good . . . alternate. In case he needed one."

She stood up, shade-fast, and began pacing around the room. All right, it was less of a pace and more of a furious clomp.

"He . . . he *tricked* me . . ." she ranted, yanking at her hair. "He lied, and-and-he—" Sloane had never seen her this upset. A big part of him wanted to stand, to try to hold her, but that wasn't what she needed right now.

So he let her curse and mutter, in an ever-widening circle around the room. Sloane didn't intervene until she spun around and punched a concrete wall.

"Rags!" He jumped up and raced over to her, cradling her hand. The skin on her knuckles had split, and he could swear he'd heard a couple of bones in her fingers fracture. She was staring down at it in grim fascination. The concrete, meanwhile, had cracked and dented.

When she finally met his eyes, the look in them was frightening. "I need you to call whatever contacts you have," she said in a perfectly calm voice. "You might need to mesmerize one of the BPI employees. We need to find Sieglinde."

He blinked at her for a moment. "Why?"

"Because we are switching fucking sides."

Chapter 15

IN THE EXCITEMENT OF getting away from the brownstone, Lindy had forgotten all about Chase's cryptic instructions to meet later. "I'm assuming you don't mean the *actual* White House, in DC," she replied.

"A little yes, but mostly no," Alex said cheerfully. "Back when Chase and I were just out of the academy, we took a road trip across the country to visit Chase's sister at the University of Wisconsin. We stopped in Chicago for a couple of days, and walked around downtown. Navy Pier, the Loop, all that tourist stuff."

"Okay . . ." Lindy had wandered around that area a few times herself, but there were plenty of white buildings there.

"The *Chicago-Tribune* building has this thing where they've inserted stones from famous buildings and monuments into the exterior walls," he explained. "There's a piece from the Berlin Wall, from the House of Parliament—"

"And one from the White House," Lindy supplied, getting it.

"Yeah. Chase and I joked that if we got separated, or if one of us went home with a girl, we would meet the next morning at the White House." He shrugged. "I had forgotten about it until he said that this morning."

They fought tourist traffic into the Loop, where Alex paid a ridiculous amount of money to park Noelle's Prius in a garage near Tribune Tower. Lindy was surprised at how full the garage was, but a lot of people probably came into the city from the suburbs for dinner and a show.

When they finally found a parking spot, Alex turned to her and said seriously, "Lindy . . . I think you should drink some of my blood."

Lindy had to smile. He was just so solemn about it. "I can make it to tonight. I'll . . . find someone."

"But I'm right here," Alex insisted. "And I don't mind."

She gave him a skeptical look, but Alex just said, "Really. It'd be easier than worrying about you."

Lindy sighed. "Fine." She hated to admit it, but she needed to feed soon or she was going to be useless.

Now that she'd agreed, though, she could hear Alex's pulse pick up. "Okay, how do . . . how does this work?"

"Usually," she intoned, "I would romance you with a bottle of wine, get your shirt off, mesmerize you to believe you're having an orgasm, then bite your neck with my two perfect canines."

"Really?"

Lindy laughed. "No."

"Well, I don't know," he said, injured.

"Give me your hand."

Alex put his hand in hers, and she turned it over, looking at his veins. She glanced around. The parking garage was deserted. They'd parked as far from any cameras as possible, but still.

"Okay." Lindy leaned over and kissed him, putting their still-joined hands in his lap. "If anyone asks," she said very seriously, "I'm just giving you a blow job."

While he was still laughing, she bent her head and bit into the back of his hand where it lay on his leg. It would hurt, since she couldn't mesmerize him, but only a little. And the shade saliva would still help him heal quickly.

~

Alex had wanted Lindy to stay in the car while he met Chase, to minimize the amount of time she spent in the sun, but she insisted on coming with him. Most of the downtown businesses weren't operating, but there were plenty of tourists on the streets. The two of them held hands and walked casually, like they were out for a stroll, though Alex kept a close eye on the crowd. He wasn't about to put anything past Hector at this point.

They reached the White House stone a few minutes before four, and stopped awkwardly on the sidewalk to wait. People milled past them, and Alex pulled out the burner phone and pretended to take a selfie with the White House stone, just to have something to do.

After ten minutes Alex began to worry. What if Chase was still in custody? It had seemed like Palmer was willing to play ball, but could he have kept Chase in questioning just to spite them? Did he decide to use Chase as bait for Hector?

Lindy squeezed his hand, understanding his concern, but there was nothing to do but wait.

At 4:19, though, Alex heard a familiar voice calling his name, and turned to see Chase rushing along the sidewalk toward them. His hair was damp, and his clothes looked fresh.

"Sorry I'm late," he said as he hurried up. "I had to take a shower. It was dire."

Alex embraced him, squeezing hard with relief. "Good to see you, brother," he said, then pulled back to look at Chase. There were wrinkles in his clothing, like they'd just come out of a package. Alex noticed a tag on one sleeve and yanked it free.

"Oh, thanks." Chase glanced down at himself, looking for other tags. "I didn't want to go back to my place, since Hector obviously knows it, so I hit a Banana Republic and stopped at my gym to clean up."

"You look good. Better than yesterday."

Alex glanced at Lindy, who just said, "Hey, Chase? Hop on one foot."

Chase looked puzzled. "Why—oh. Nah. I'm good."

She smiled at him then. "All right, then. How's my cat?"

"Sarah is looking after her," he replied. Sarah Greer was the very capable office manager for the BPI pod. "She called me to check in, and really wanted to do something to help."

"Thank you," Lindy said.

"Can we—" Chase began, but then a man in sunglasses and a ball cap came toward them in a straight line, from behind Lindy. Both Alex and Chase rested a hand on their weapons. She followed their gazes and turned around just as the man touched the tip of his ball cap, his eyes on her. This was Sloane, the asshole who worked for Reagan. Alex had seen a photo.

"Afternoon, my lady. Gents."

Lindy reacted well before either BPI agent. She grabbed the lapels of Sloane's jacket and whirled him into the side of Tribune Tower, his head smacking the wall with a sickening *crack* only inches from the chunk of White House.

"How did you find us?" she demanded.

"Easy, my lady, easy." Sloane raised his hands, as though whether or not he was armed would make a difference.

"My lady?" Alex muttered, but the people around them were stopping to look. "It's fine," Alex said loudly, but his scarred face didn't seem to comfort the onlookers.

Sloane made a show of smiling and moving his head to show he wasn't hurt. "Just a disagreement," he called.

With a last round of odd looks, the crowd began moving again. Lindy hadn't let go of his jacket. "*How?*" she said fiercely. She was glaring at Sloane with such intensity that Alex half-expected the other shade to burst into flames.

"Reagan called the FBI office pretending to be your secretary," Sloane rushed to say. "No one knew where you were, but they said Chase Eddy was just about to leave the interview rooms. I followed him here."

Alex glanced at Chase, who flushed. "Well, that's embarrassing."

"Don't sweat it, mate," Sloane said to him. "I've been doing this a while."

"Is Reagan with you?" Lindy asked. She still hadn't released Sloane.

"No. I wanted to talk to you first."

Slowly, Lindy uncurled her fingers from Sloane's jacket. The other shade eased himself away from the wall, as though he were still expecting an attack. When none came, he brushed at his jacket and straightened his Cubs cap, trying a smile.

Lindy just glared at him. "What about?"

"Er, can we talk somewhere a bit more private?" Sloane said. "There's apologizing to do, and some arse-kissing."

"What does that mean?" Alex asked.

"It means," Sloane said, smiling, "Reagan and I, we find ourselves suddenly and deeply invested in helping you lot kill Hector."

Chapter 16

THEY FOUND A CLUSTER of public benches, and Sloane began to talk. And talk. Eventually, Alex was satisfied that he was telling the truth. He could tell Lindy still had her doubts, but they were short on ideas, and their forty-eight hours were ticking down quickly. She agreed to give collaboration a shot.

Chase went to rent a car—Lindy didn't think Hector had much pull with credit card companies; he was more of a hands-on asshole—and the three of them met up with a contrite, and nearly silent, Reagan. By the time everyone was headed for the rental cabin, it was just after sunset.

Alex drove, with a watchful eye on Lindy, who sat sideways in the passenger seat so she could glare daggers at Reagan in the back. Sloane occasionally tried to crack a joke, but the tension in the small car was impenetrable, and even he eventually gave up. Alex found himself wishing he could have ridden with Chase—but then Lindy might have killed one of the other shades. She was obviously still pissed about Reagan shooting her with meth.

"What did you do with Aidan and Cooper?" Lindy asked Reagan.

The young woman had been staring at her hands, but now she straightened her shoulders and met Lindy's stare. "I left them some money and instructions to get to a friend in St. Louis," she said. "He'll look after them when . . . until this is over."

Sloane was looking at Reagan now too. "You didn't tell them goodbye?"

The young shade shook her head. "Coop would have tried to help, and Aidan probably would have tagged along. This isn't their fight." She hesitated for just a moment, then added, "And they'd both be a liability."

Lindy didn't respond, but the answer seemed to satisfy her. They rode silently for the rest of the way.

~

At the cabin, Lindy waited in the car with the other two shades while Alex went in first, to warn Hadley and Ruiz. He found his two young agents collapsed at kitchen chairs, looking exhausted.

"Did you bring food?" Ruiz said hopefully.

Alex dropped a Culver's bag on the small kitchen table, and Ruiz had his cheeseburger unwrapped and in his mouth with terrifying speed. Before Alex could tell them about Sloane and Reagan, Hadley burst out, "We've got *nothing*, boss. If we had access to recognition software or some fingerprint samples, that might be one thing, but this whole thing is just dead ends." She waved at the wall with a look of disapproval, as though it had personally failed to meet her expectations. Lindy had talked them through some of it on the phone, but unfortunately she hadn't kept in contact with any of Hector's associates. Alex understood why, but this would have been a hell of a lot easier if they could just track down even one henchman.

"Did you try the Dark Net?" he asked.

"Yes, and I used the login stuff Lindy texted," Hadley replied. After popping three French fries in her mouth, she seemed to have forgotten the food. "There hasn't been any chatter since our first clash with Hector at that dental clinic. It's like a bunch of prairie dogs who ran into their holes."

"Vampire prairie dogs," Ruiz supplied.

"Yes, thank you."

"Well, I've got a couple of new suspects for you to interview," Alex offered.

Ruiz sort of brightened, but Hadley just looked suspicious. "Thing is," Alex continued, "you have to promise not to shoot them."

"At least, not right away," Lindy said from the doorway. She turned sideways so Sloane and Reagan could enter.

Sloane attempted a smile. "Hi, all," he said cheerfully. "We're here for the assassination committee? Oh, whoa."

Both Hadley and Ruiz had scooted their chairs from the table and reached for their weapons. Sloane immediately angled his body so it was between Reagan and the guns, but Alex raised his hands. "Whoa, guys," he said. "They want to help us get Hector."

"Why do you think you can trust them?" Hadley replied immediately. It was not an unreasonable question, but Alex let Sloane answer.

"If we wished any of you harm," he pointed out, "we could have done that by now."

"You could have tried," Lindy muttered behind him.

Reagan stepped forward, raising her chin. "Hector lied to me," she said clearly. "He told me he was going to unite the shades, to give us a leader. I didn't know until this morning that he was planning to do it through fear." She shook her head. "Terrorizing humans is not the way to peace."

"Hector doesn't care about peace," Lindy snapped. "He just wants power. And recognition."

"I didn't know that," Reagan said, her voice a little

weak. "Just like I didn't know that he was the one who transmuted me."

Hadley's eyes widened, but Alex's thoughts spun off in a different direction. "Recognition," he repeated thoughtfully.

Lindy's head turned toward him. "Tell me you have an idea."

"Hmm."

"Don't worry," Chase assured her. "That's definitely his I-have-an-idea face."

"Uh-huh. How long before he tells us about this idea?" Hadley asked.

Chase shushed her. "Don't derail him. You'll scare it away."

Alex ignored all this and focused on Lindy. "You said Hector wants recognition, specifically from you—and he wants everyone to think he's the once and future king of the shades. Right?"

She nodded. Alex said, "It must have really pissed him off when we caught him killing teenagers and put his name on the news."

"It really did." This was from Reagan, who still looked rueful. "He rants about it all the time. I'm not sure he even means to send out those thoughts, but they bleed through."

"Okay." Alex nodded to himself. "Okay. Right now, Hector is stirring things up without claiming responsibility, getting the humans into a panic and making the shades nervous about persecution. Presumably he's going to push everyone toward riots in the streets, and then he'll swoop in and save the day as the recognized shade leader. He's hoping Lindy gets blamed for it, but really that's just a bonus." He looked at Lindy. "Lindy, how many humans know exactly what you look like? Besides the people in this room."

She blinked hard. "Um. Sarah, Palmer, and Noelle. A few people from my old office in Cincinnati, but they didn't know I'm a shade." Her eyes went distant for a second as she really thought it over. "The federal agent who drove us to the airport in Cincinnati."

He'd been right—she had never met Harding in person. There was a photo of Lindy in the FBI database, for her ID, but it was slightly blurry—he had suspected her of moving a little at just the right moment. Alex felt himself lighten for the first time since he'd woken up in Lindy's bed.

"Okay, dude," Chase said impatiently. "What are you thinking?"

Alex grinned. "Hector wants the world's shades to just voluntarily place him on this imaginary throne, right?"

"Yeah . . ."

"So I'm thinking we steal the imaginary throne right out from underneath him."

Chapter 17

ALEX EXPLAINED THE IDEA, and proposed sort of a loose plan. They all kicked it around for another half an hour, revising and filling in details, while Hadley ate her cheeseburger and Ruiz covertly stole most of her French fries.

Finally, Chase scrubbed the back of his head with his palm. "Alex, man," he said. "I've been on board with many a harebrained plan of yours, but this is by far the most harebrained."

"That's not a no," Alex replied. He was looking at Lindy, who seemed to be suppressing a smile.

"It's crazy," she told him. "And kind of stupid. But I like it."

She turned to Reagan, and her expression hardened. "But this whole thing is pretty much riding on you. You get that, right?"

Reagan, for her part, looked properly terrified. "Yeah."

Lindy softened, but only a little. "On the other hand, if we can pull this off, you get everything you want. That has to feel good."

"Not quite as good as I thought it would," the younger shade admitted.

Sloane squeezed her hand. "You'll do great."

Reagan gave him a surprised look, and Alex realized that the young woman had no idea Sloane was in love with her. Jesus. Even *he* knew that.

"We need a reporter," Hadley said thoughtfully, pulling them back on track. "Preferably someone national, but willing to come here."

"Hector wants us to go to the East Coast, so that's the last thing we're gonna do," Lindy explained to the other shades. "We set a trap here."

Hadley looked at her fellow BPI agents. "Do any of you have contacts?"

There was a moment of silence, and then Chase raised his hand, looking a little sheepish. "I dated someone at CNN in New York," he explained. To Alex, he added, "Remember Felicity Watts?"

Alex raised an eyebrow. "Is she still speaking to you?"

"Of course," Chase said, feigning insult.

Sloane looked amused. "Bit of a ladies' man, are we?" he said to Chase. Ruiz snickered.

"Get her on the phone," Alex told Chase. "Find out how soon she can get someone to Chicago."

Chase pulled out his cell phone and headed for the cabin door. While Chase was making the call, Alex turned to the rest of them. "Assuming phase one works—"

Sloane rolled his eyes. "Are we really calling it phase one?"

"Assuming phase one works," Alex continued, with great dignity, "we need a location for the actual trap. Something contained, but as far away from civilians as possible."

"Somewhere out in the country?" Ruiz suggested.

Lindy shook her head. "He's as comfortable there as anywhere else. Woods, open land, rocky cliffs—anything you've got around here, we've lived in it at some point."

Sloane started to speak, but Lindy was tilting her head to the side, thinking. "Hold on," she said. "He does dislike water. Maybe something near a beach, or an island?"

"How *much* does he dislike water?" Alex asked.

She shrugged. "He almost drowned when we were children. He'd be fine on a boat or anywhere his feet can touch, but he hates deep water. If that helps."

"The water cribs," Hadley said suddenly.

They all looked at her, and Alex said, "The what now?"

"Ruiz, do you have that Chicago map?"

Ruiz handed her a street map of Chicago. Hadley unfolded it and slid a couple of blank pieces of paper under the edge that represented Lake Michigan. She consulted her phone, and kept talking as she drew on the paper.

"We learned about them in school. In Chicago we get our water from Lake Michigan—but during the mid-nineteenth century, the city also dumped sewage in the river, and the river dumped it into the lake. People got sick. So they came up with a plan to build a structure way off the shoreline that would protect the water from pollution. Kind of like a circular stone fence." She drew some small circles, with lines connecting them to shore. "Then the structure was connected to the city via underground pipes.

"This is rough, but you get the idea." She lifted her hand, and Alex could see that she'd drawn a bunch of circles at various points offshore, with little names beside each one. He counted ten of them. "They called them water cribs, because they protect the water like the walls of a crib protect a baby," Hadley went on. "The first one was Two-Mile Crib, then Four-Mile Crib, and then they named a bunch after prominent Chicagoans. The point is, they're like tiny man-made islands, and you can only get to them by boat."

"Are they still operating?" Alex asked. "I don't want to mess with the city's actual water supply."

"Let's see." Hadley consulted an article on her phone. "Yeah, looks like two of them are still in operation. Of the other eight, though, a bunch of them have been demolished, and one, the Lawrence Avenue Crib, is now surrounded by Lincoln Park. But these two"—she pointed to two of the circles—"are still standing, and abandoned."

It sounded promising, at least. "Do we have satellite images?" Alex asked.

Ruiz opened the laptop, and pecked out the Google Earth website with his index fingers. "Let me," Hadley said, sliding the laptop toward herself. After a moment she looked up at Alex. "The commercial mapping satellites don't display that far off the coast."

"That might not be a bad thing," Alex mused. "If we can't see it, neither can Hector. Are there people out there?"

"Not really," Hadley said. "In the nineties everything was automated. The Coast Guard patrols out there to make sure some idiot civilians don't trespass on the cribs, but that's about it."

"I might be able to talk Gil into backing off the Coast Guard," Alex said. He looked at the map again. "Which one of the inactive cribs is the newest?"

She glanced at her phone, and tapped a circle on the map. "This one, the Jane M. Byrne Crib. It was built in 1948."

"Let's focus on that one," Alex said. "It's probably the least likely to kill us."

"How will Hector know where to find us?" Hadley asked.

"As soon as we get to the water crib I'll turn the phone on," Lindy replied. "If he doesn't track the phone or call me, I'll call him."

"And what, challenge him to a duel?" Ruiz said, sounding more curious than anything else.

Lindy wasn't offended. "Something like that. I'd bet that he's tracking the phone he left at Roza's house. I think that was part of the point of killing her, so he could both taunt us and find me. So we'll use that against him."

Alex glanced around the room. "The wi-fi's surprisingly good here. Anyone else have a laptop or tablet?"

Sloane raised an index finger. Alex nodded. "I want you and Hadley to work on getting me as much information on the Byrne crib as possible. Blueprints, anecdotal descriptions, photos, anything. Drive into town and buy a printer if you need it. I've got some cash."

Chase came back into the cabin, and Alex looked over at him. "She'll do it," he said. "She's gonna bring a whole team, and she said if I'm lying or wrong . . ." He cleared his throat. "Well. Bad things. But they'll be on the next flight."

"Good. In the meantime, I want you and Ruiz to go back to Noelle and see what she has for us. Ruiz can fill you in on water cribs on the way." He paused, then added, "And you better check with Palmer and see how he's coming on getting methamphetamine. You guys might need to knock over a shitkicker bar in Wisconsin or something."

Ruiz did a fist pump.

"Do you want me to go with them?" Reagan offered, pushing her dark hair behind her ears. "I can help with the, uh, Wisconsin shitkickers."

Alex shook his head. "They can handle it. You and Lindy need to get ready for tomorrow morning."

He shot Lindy a quick look, but she just nodded. Apparently her ice wall of Reagan hatred was starting to thaw. "Okay," Alex said. "I'm going to see about getting us some boats. Let's get moving."

might need to knock over a snickicker bar in Wisconsin or something.

Ruiz did a fist pump.

"Do you want me to go with them?" Reagan offered, pushing her dark hair behind her ears. "I can help with the uh, Wisconsin snickickers."

Alex shook his head. "They can handle it. You and Lindy need to get ready for tomorrow morning."

He shot Lindy a quick look, but she just nodded. Apparently her the wall of Reagan barred was starting to thaw. "Okay," Alex said. "I'm going to see about getting us some beans. Let's get moving."

Chapter 18

GABRIEL RUIZ FOLLOWED AGENT Eddy out to the SUV he'd rented earlier in the day, feeling some trepidation. He didn't mind the assignment itself, but being with Eddy worried him. Ruiz had been mesmerized by Hector's people on two separate occasions, and it had really fucked up his head both times. What would it be like to have Hector mesmerizing you nearly every day, for weeks? Could Hector have left some kind of time-release order in Eddy's mind? Was he going to suddenly flip out?

"Maybe I should drive," Ruiz offered.

Eddy just shrugged and tossed him the keys, but when they were seated in the SUV, the younger agent turned to him. As assistant SAC, Eddy technically outranked him, but Ruiz had almost two decades of experience on him, and Eddy was usually pretty mindful of that.

"Just so you know," Eddy said, "Lindy thinks I'm in the clear. It's been too long since Hector last mesmerized me. There's no way I can still be under his influence."

"I wasn't worried about it," Ruiz lied. "But . . . good to know."

~

They got ensnared in the Saturday-night traffic as they drove back into the city, and Ruiz found himself desperately wishing for some bubble lights and a siren. By the time they made it to Noelle Liang's office, Ruiz was worried about her even being there. "You think she went home?" he said. "It's getting late."

Chase shook his head with confidence, and Ruiz remembered he and the engineer had been friends before any of this. "Trust me, she's still there."

They didn't have a shade with them to grease the wheels, so they had to go in the front of the building and show their IDs to the security guard. As far as Ruiz knew, being on suspension pending inquiry wasn't enough to bar them from going into the building to visit a friend. This was more or less what Eddy told the security guard, who scrutinized their IDs carefully but let them sign in.

Ruiz hadn't been to Liang's lab before—he hadn't even met the woman—but apparently Eddy and Noelle were pals, because he led Ruiz down the twisting hallways with no hesitation. But when he twisted the knob on the door marked "Liang, Noelle," Ruiz heard the lock engage. Since Chase Eddy was technically his superior, he refrained from saying, "I told you so."

"That's weird." Eddy frowned and knocked on the

door. "You hear that?"

Ruiz leaned closer, and heard some kind of foreign pop music practically vibrating through the door. "Liang!" he yelled, pounding on the door with a closed fist.

The music went down, and they heard someone unlocking the door. It opened a crack, and a woman's face peered in the gap. She had black hair chopped in an asymmetrical pixie cut and safety pins lining her white lab coat for no apparent reason. "Chase?" Her gaze shifted to Ruiz and back. "Who's this?"

"This is Gabriel Ruiz. He's part of our pod."

"Oh, okay. Hi-Gabriel-I'm-Noelle," she said in a rush. "Come in, quick."

"What the hell is going—" Chase started to say, but Liang was practically yanking them inside, closing and locking the door behind them. Ruiz and Eddy both looked around the room and gaped.

The space was huge, with rows of tables sort of like in a college science lab. At one table a city cop was sitting in front of a stack of paperwork, holding a pen. She was white, with a close-cropped haircut and her badge hanging on a chain around her neck. She barely glanced up when they arrived. Special Agent Gil Palmer was sitting in the back left corner of the room at a big metal desk, wearing what looked like noise-canceling headphones.

His arms were crossed over his chest, and he appeared to be fast asleep.

Then there was the back right quarter of the lab, which had been sectioned off with enormous sheets of thick plastic, like the kind used on construction sites. One flap was held open with wooden clothespins, exposing a weaselly-looking man in cutoff shorts and a T-shirt with the sleeves ripped off. He was wearing goggles and thick rubber gloves, and waved uncertainly as they walked in. His eyes were darting between them and the city cop.

Eddy said it first. "Noelle . . . what the hell's going on?"

"Oh! Right. Sorry, I've had a lot of coffee. About . . . a lot. Introductions!" She clapped her hands and led them over to the cop's table, like a tour guide presenting a new specimen. "*This* is my friend Liz Bassett, she's a CPD narcotics detective. Palmer you already know—I'd wake him up, but we *just* got him down for his nap—and the walking stereotype in the back is Ricky Martin—his actual name, by the way, no relation to the singer, and don't ask him why he insists on going by Ricky instead of Rich or Richard because that conversation is twenty minutes of nowhere." She paused to take a breath, and finished with, "Ricky cooks meth."

"*Used to* cook meth," the weaselly man corrected. He hadn't objected to Noelle's characterization of him, but that might have been because she was talking too fast for him to understand. "I'm coming out of retirement for one night only."

"Sure, Ricky," said Liz Bassett. She nodded at Ruiz and Eddy. "He's one of my CIs," she explained.

"You have a *meth lab* going in an FBI building?" Eddy looked scandalized, which would have been a little funny if Ruiz didn't feel the same.

"Get back to work, Ricky!" Noelle called over her shoulder. The cook grumbled something at her, but he pulled the clothespin and went back into his sectioned-off area. Then she turned back to them. "Yeah, well, I realized I couldn't have just *any* methamphetamine—I need high-quality materials for my experiments. Who knows what kind of shit these local rednecks put in their drugs? So Ricky's been teaching me how to make it. It's not that hard, really. I mean, the instructions are on the internet, but Ricky's actually been a pretty good resource, once you get past the body odor."

"He's a good cook, you gotta say that for him," Bassett agreed, without looking up from her report forms. She finished one page and flipped it over, pulling the next one closer to her. "Ricky's problem is that he's *only* good at cooking meth."

"Plus the name thing, that's definitely a second problem," Ruiz pointed out.

"You're on board with all of this?" Eddy asked the city

cop. He still looked incredulous.

Bassett finally looked up, her eyes narrowing a little. "On board? *Hell,* no. But I know Noelle. If she calls me and asks for a cook, that means she's going to keep going until she finds one." Bassett shrugged. "Ricky's kind of a shit, but he's harmless. I can't say that for most of the cooks I bust."

"Plus, I'm gonna make it up to you," Noelle promised, winking at Bassett. The cop smiled back, and it was not a platonic smile. Ruiz and Eddy exchanged a look that pretty much just said, *Oh.*

Chase cleared his throat. "What's happening with the guns?" he said instead.

"That's under control. Come this way." Noelle led them to a table full of . . . gun parts? Ruiz recognized a lot of the pieces, but everything was disassembled, and some of it just didn't look right.

"These used to be pretty standard dart guns, the kind they use in zoos and nature preserves," Noelle explained, seeing his confusion. "But I tested them—no, not on Palmer; I swear he fell asleep on his own—and the range is only about seventy yards, plus I think it's too slow for shades." She shrugged. "Basically, if you're close enough to shoot, they'll already be aware of you. So I've been souping it up." She pointed to the next table, which held a single modified long gun. "That's my prototype.

Cartridge-fired, rather than CO2, takes a five-round clip. I think it's enough of an improvement, but it's hard to be sure without—" She turned to them, brightening. "Wait, can you get a shade to help me test this? Just the dart gun, not the actual meth. I mean, I know we all like Lindy . . ."

The two men looked at each other. Eddy gave him a tiny smile, and Ruiz knew they were on the same page. "But we don't like Sloane," he said under his breath.

"I think we can work that out," Eddy told her. "What about sidearms?"

"For those I have to do CO2-fired," she said. "I've got the original dart guns ready for modification, I just wanted to perfect the long gun first, since you guys will have a better shot—sorry, accidental pun—from a distance. It's all under control," she said again.

Ruiz glanced around again, taking in improvised meth lab, the gun parts, the hyper engineer, the sleeping federal agent. Sure. Under control.

Chapter 19

ANDY KETTMAN PACED AROUND the control room, fuming in his immaculate Tom Ford suit.

For the last twelve years, Kettman had been the anchor of the Chicago segment of CNN's flagship Sunday-morning program. It didn't sound like much, but his segments were shown live for nearly the full eight o'clock hour in the greater Chicagoland area, and his clips were often part of the ten o'clock national show, where they had a major impact—or at least, that was what he told himself.

But now, Kettman's entire morning program had been usurped by some twentysomething skirt with bouncy red hair and even bouncier ... well. Everything on her was bouncy, really.

Kettman spun around and did another pacing circuit of the room, glaring at Mary Lynn Toogan, his senior producer. She was chewing a cuticle and studiously ignoring his tantrum, which made Kettman even angrier. The whole control room was filled with hushed whispering, but not about him: about some mystery guest who was supposed to be *so* important. Whoever he was, he got to come in ten seconds before they started rolling, with no makeup or anything.

But, Kettman reasoned, how important could this guy be, if they'd given his desk to this Felicity Watson or Watzo or whatever it was? He cocked his head then, brightening a little. Maybe they were interviewing some notorious lech, and Felicity had been brought in to tempt him? That would be good TV . . . but if that was the case, why not just *tell* Kettman?

His thoughts went around and around like that for three more circuits of the back of the room, and then suddenly, the whole place went silent.

The mystery guest had finally walked onto the stage. One of the interns had pulled up a second rolling chair, and she was taking a seat behind the desk—*his* desk.

It was just some chick.

Kettman snorted loudly, some of his fury abating. *That* was why they'd brought in this girl from the New York desk? Because the ladies wanted to stick together?

Maybe, he realized, it was actually a good thing that he wasn't behind the desk. This interview would probably be dull, and pulling a baby reporter from New York to take the fall could only help him.

Relaxing a little, Kettman studied the guest. She didn't look like much, just another young woman with styled blond hair, black heels, and a nicely tailored dress. Okay, maybe she did look kind of fierce and centered, like she was on a battlefield about to deliver a rousing speech. But there was no reason for his whole station to get all worked up about it.

Felicity looked nervous, giving the guest a wide berth. Further proof that she didn't deserve this job. Kettman rolled his eyes to himself. "I'm getting out of here," he announced as Felicity did her "breaking news" intro. No one in the control room so much as looked up. He stormed toward the exit and was already twisting the door handle when the guest spoke.

"Thank you, Felicity," she said. "My name is Rosalind Frederick, and I'm a shade."

All around the room, cameramen and interns gasped. Kettman's hand slid from the knob as though it were greased. He spun around to see that everyone was looking at Mary Lynn, who just spoke quietly into her mic. She wasn't chewing the cuticle anymore.

The young woman at the desk continued, "I am not, however, your enemy." She paused for a minute to let that sink in. "And I have not mesmerized anyone in order to be here. I simply felt it was necessary to address you, the

American people, about yesterday's attacks on the Bureau of Preternatural Investigations."

"Thank you, Ms. Frederick," Felicity said smoothly. "I can confirm that I was first contacted over the phone, where there was no possibility of being mesmerized. But with all respect, how can our viewers be certain you're telling the truth about being a shade? After all, many people have come forward over the last year and claimed to be—"

"A bloodsucking vampire?" the chick answered. She smiled. "Yes, of course. You've seen the footage of Ambrose's stimulation response in Camp Vamp, correct?"

"Yes, of course." Felicity looked too sure of herself. This part had obviously been prearranged. On the screen behind her, the technicians would be bringing up a still image of Ambrose with his eyes all red.

"And I am told your station was able to secure some blood from a local butcher?"

"Yes." Now a hint of uncertainty flickered across Felicity's face. "Will that . . . will it work?"

"To feed me? No. I can't get everything my body needs from cow or pig's blood." The woman made a face. "Believe me, I've tried. But it should still provoke the creepy red eye thing."

Felicity couldn't help but smile at the phrasing, and most of the control room smiled with her. She motioned off stage, and an intern dressed in black hurried forward with a clear glass beaker filled with red liquid. Kettman could just imagine the hurried conversation they must have had that morning over what kind of container to use. A glass would be too cavalier. Tupperware too informal. He had to admit, a beaker did seem appropriate. It was what he would have chosen.

Felicity accepted the beaker and set it warily on the table in between herself and the guest. The young woman snaked out a hand and slid the glass toward herself.

The red began bleeding into her eyes while it was still nearly an arm's length away. There were gasps and muted cries in the control room as the girl took a sniff of the beaker and turned her face toward the camera. Her eyes were completely scarlet from one lid to another. Kettman felt his insides loosen with primal fear.

"I trust I've made the point?" the guest said, her voice a bit strangled.

"Yes, yes," Felicity said hurriedly. "Can I . . ."

The shade—holy shit, she really *was* a shade—slid the glass back toward the anchor, who passed it to the same intern, who took off at a trot, probably to dump it down the sink. Kettman had to admit—to himself; never out loud—that this Felicity chick had some balls on her, getting a shade worked up while she was sitting two feet away. As it was, half the newsroom might end up suing

Mary Lynn for putting them at risk.

"I hope you understand why we needed to ask that of you," Felicity was saying to the shade.

"I do. But I'd like to move on, if we could." The chick blinked rapidly a few more times, and her eyes had returned to brown. "Most importantly, I want to speak to you about the shade who killed or ordered the killings of sixteen humans yesterday. His name is Hector."

The control room was completely silent, save for the low hum of the equipment. This was Chicago; they'd reported on the BPI's pursuit of Hector nearly two months earlier. The chick might as well have said "the boogeyman."

"For quite some time now," the woman continued, "shades have been without leadership. Yesterday, Hector exploited this scarcity and convinced a handful of shades to help him break into the detention facility commonly known as Camp Vamp. As a result, innocent people died."

The young woman paused to take a breath. "And I bear some responsibility for this mess, because I created the vacuum that made it possible."

Felicity saw her chance to insert herself. "What do you mean by that, Ms. Frederick?"

The girl flashed a smile at the news anchor. Kettman had to admit, it was a pretty good smile. "You can call me Rosalind. To answer your question, my original name was Sieglinde. I was born in Gaul—the area we now call western Germany—in the year of our Lord, seven hundred and two."

This time even Felicity gasped, but the young woman wasn't done. "I am, I believe, the oldest living shade on the planet. I am also a direct descendant of Rainer, the first king of vampires."

She turned her head to look directly at the camera. "What I'm saying, Felicity, is that I am the queen of vampires, and today I take back my throne."

It should have sounded ludicrous—the queen of vampires?—but Kettman felt his insides go cold. She absolutely radiated confidence and sincerity. Not just that—there was an edge of danger coming off her, too. Even if he'd been tempted to laugh, he would have been way too scared.

Felicity must have had a similar reaction, because she just sat there for a second. Kettman realized she hadn't known about the royalty thing. She probably just thought she was getting an exclusive with the world's first admitted free shade.

Damn, he wanted it to be him.

The woman calling herself Rosalind Frederick gave a tiny, rueful smile that took some of the starch out of her words. "Okay, that sounded really dramatic, didn't it? Are you all right, Felicity? You still with me?"

The young news anchor gave a little start and said in a small voice, "Yes, of course. I'm sorry. Do you . . . should I ask questions now?"

The shade gave a small laugh that cut some of the tension, but then her face grew serious. "I'm happy to answer some questions in a moment, Felicity, but first, let me add this." She looked straight in the camera again. "After yesterday's events, I want to make it clear that no shade shall kill a human being without repercussion, ever again. I will personally make sure of it."

"What about the legal aspect?" Felicity said tentatively. "The federal government hasn't decided whether or not you have the same rights as—um, human beings."

The shade smiled in a way that was both sweet and menacing, and Kettman found himself taking an involuntary step away from her. Who *was* this chick? "I realize that the United States Congress has been stymied on this issue," Rosalind said, "but if they'll have me, I plan to travel to Washington and work to create legislature that protects *both* of our kinds." She paused, looking away from Felicity and right into the camera. "Right after I devote my considerable resources to helping the BPI apprehend Hector."

"Do you know him?" Felicity blurted, then immediately looked sort of chastised. "I mean, I'm not suggesting all shades know each other—"

"That's all right," the shade said gently. "Yes, I know Hector. We were transmuted at the same time. But although he and I have personal history, we do *not* share the same ideas about the future relationship between humans and shades."

"Can you expand on that?"

The shade nodded. "The people who oppose shades, many of whom were protesting in the streets of Washington yesterday, say that we're parasites. Hector would like you to think we are a superior specimen, an evolved form of humanity. But neither concept is actually correct. Shades and humans are a symbiotic species, which means you need us as much as we need you."

"How?" Felicity asked, then tried to soften it. "I mean, pardon me, ma'am, but how do humans need shades?"

"Our saliva contains an immunity boost that prevents humanity from spreading pandemics and plagues, and slows or even stops many cancers and other illnesses," the woman replied.

Felicity gave her a thoughtful nod, one of the essential tools in any news anchor's toolbox. "As you know, ma'am, most states, including this one, have made the consumption of human blood illegal. What will you do if the government arrests you before you can stop Hector?"

"Oh, I have already been working with the government," the shade said sweetly. "A few minutes before the broadcast, my attorney emailed your producer documents from the Department of Justice, securing my official employment as a consultant. They already know who I am, and what I can do."

"Then why are we just hearing from you now?" Felicity pressed. Kettman had to kind of admire the kid for that one.

The shade looked regretful. "Until now, I felt I could be most useful behind the scenes, working under the public's radar. Unfortunately, Hector has forced my hand."

Felicity nodded. "All right. I understand that the BPI and the Department of Justice have acknowledged you, but what if the Illinois government tries to detain you?"

"If that does happen, I will submit to arrest. I have no intention of going to war against the government." Kettman wasn't sure how she did it, but the words *even though I would win* somehow hung in the air without being spoken.

The shade turned to face the camera again, as though to speak to the governor of Illinois himself. "But I would remind you that there is no evidence of my breaking any laws. More importantly, I may be the only one strong enough to stop the monster at your door."

There was an uneasy pause, and Kettman could see

everyone in the newsroom easing away, glancing at the door. She was that menacing.

Then the pretty shade turned and gave Felicity a sunny smile. "I would be happy to answer some of your questions now."

~

Twenty minutes later, Kettman was still sitting on a stool in the control room, sipping from a bottle of water and marveling at the turn of events.

Part of him was still wounded and envious that he hadn't been the one to break the story. At the same time, though, the newscaster in him, the one who used to spend his time obsessing over journalistic integrity rather than Armani suits, had stirred back to life. Kettman was proud—proud of Felicity, proud of the Chicago news station, proud of his network. They had blown the lid off the world. This day would be talked about for the rest of time, and by God, he'd been here.

Hey, maybe he could talk Mary Lynn into giving him an associate producer credit. Least she could do, really.

As the broadcast team wrapped up, Kettman found himself wanting to approach this Lindy, to shake her hand and thank her for coming forward. Okay, fine, maybe he just wanted to preen a little, to show that he could be the noble guy who'd stepped aside for the good of a story.

But the moment the cameras turned off, the young woman immediately began detaching the microphone cord from her shirt, already moving toward the door. All around her, interns and production assistants were edging away, trying to keep themselves away from the scary vampire lady.

"Oh!" she said, turning back to Felicity. "Almost forgot."

She pulled an earbud out of her air, the same kind the anchors used to communicate with the control room. Kettman paused. That was strange. They didn't give guests earbuds.

Who had been on the other end?

The shade reached out and grabbed Felicity's hand, shaking it enthusiastically. "Thanks a lot," she said. "I need to run now, though. Daylight and all that." She gave Felicity a wink, turned on one heel, and was gone.

~

Outside the building's side entrance, Sloane was waiting under an umbrella, the door to the rental SUV open beside him. It wasn't actually raining, but the sky was overcast again, so the people bustling past him to the building's main entrance didn't give the umbrella a second glance.

The door opened, and the shade from the interview burst through it, diving straight into the back seat. "Thank God that's over," she said sleepily, scratching at her newly blond hair. "Did you watch on your phone?"

Sloane nodded and tossed a thick canvas tarp over her. "You did great, Rags. Get some rest."

He drove around the side of the building to the main entrance, where he put the SUV in park.

A moment later, a figure in dark glasses and a brunette wig slid through the glass doors and climbed into the passenger side. "Well done," Sloane told Lindy. "You think we'll get a reaction?"

She took off the glasses and grinned at him. "I think we can count on it."

Chapter 20

COZY CONIFER CABINS
SUNDAY MORNING

AN HOUR LATER, LINDY was sitting at the kitchen table of the little rental cabin with Alex. Sloane and Reagan were resting in the only bedroom, which had been outfitted with blackout curtains and duct tape. Chase and Ruiz were napping too, on camp cots in the back of the large room. They had been at Noelle's lab until late the night before. Aside from Alex and Lindy, only Hadley was still up, and she was clearly fading, her eyelids drifting down every few minutes before she shook herself awake. Lindy had tried several times to get her to go lie down by the others, but Hadley insisted on showing them her work first.

They had been going over the sketches and photographs Hadley had collected. Beside them, the laptop was still open to CNN's website, which had been playing clips of "Rosalind's" interview nonstop.

Alex's watch beeped. "It's ten," he said, glancing down

at it. "Time to switch on the phone?"

"Yeah." Lindy went over to the counter and retrieved the cell phone that she'd brought from Roza's apartment, the one Hector had left for her. She reattached the battery and powered it up, wondering how long it would take Hector to call.

The phone rang before she even settled back into the chair. Lindy made eye contact with Alex and Hadley, who nodded that they would be quiet. She answered the phone on speaker.

"Hello?"

"You *bitch*!" her brother shouted. "What the hell are you doing?"

Across the table, Alex grinned. "Right now? Or you mean like in general?" Lindy said sweetly.

There was the sound of something breaking. "You are ruining *everything*! How dare you?"

"How *dare* I?" Lindy said, her voice rising now. "You killed innocent people, including my friend."

"You *stole her* from me!"

Lindy sighed. It was so like him to skip right over Bartell's murder to complain about her taking his toys. And that's what Reagan was to him: a toy. "I didn't have to steal her, she came to me. How long did you really think it'd be before someone told her that you were the one who turned her?"

There was a long moment of silence. "I would have told her myself, eventually," he declared. "But now you've brainwashed her, made her your stalking horse."

"So you're upset that I brainwashed her before you could?"

"You two don't even look that similar!"

This was also true—Reagan was a little scrawny and usually looked more like a guitarist in a grunge band than anything else. But dyeing her hair blond, reshaping her eyebrows, and padding her bra had helped, and as Alex had noticed the previous night, their cheekbones and the shape of their chins were actually pretty close.

Most importantly, Lindy had segregated herself from shades for decades now. Very few of them, if any, would remember exactly what she looked like, and shades changed their appearance in subtle ways all the time. As long as no one confronted Reagan physically, or noticed that she couldn't stay awake all day yet, they could get away with this indefinitely.

A voice spoke to Hector in the background, and Lindy ground her teeth. "Is that Ambrose?"

Hector was back. "Why do you care? Looking to poach more of my people?"

Lindy snorted. "Hardly. You and that little worm were made for each other. I'd never get in the way of that." Before he could respond, she added, "But I'm glad you called. I wanted to offer you a deal."

Alex raised his eyebrows at her, but Lindy gave a tiny head shake and said into his mind, *Stay with me. I need to push him a little further if we want him to come here.* "Run away," she said, echoing his words from their last call. "The United States belongs to me now."

"Is that so." His voice was soft now, and dangerous. Fear lanced through Lindy, but she pushed it away. She would *not* be afraid of her own brother. Or at least, she wouldn't let him know if she was.

"You failed, Hector," she said. "Again. And we both know you'd never win a straight fight with me. So go, lick your wounds in Romania or Luxembourg. I won't even follow you."

There was a long pause, in which the other end of the line was utterly silent. He hadn't hung up, though, and Lindy knew he was probably in a room with other shades who were suddenly terrified of the shift in Hector's mood. They were all waiting to see what he'd do.

"You want to play games, Lindy?" he said finally. "I can play games."

"You're not hearing me," Lindy said in a bored voice. "You know what your problem is, Hector? You haven't learned any new moves since 1983. It's the same boring game, and I'm tired of playing. I still have one card left, though: a real nice picture of you."

A pause. "You wouldn't." But he was just saying it. They both knew she would.

"How do you think your little minions will feel about you if I give this to the TV stations and start an international manhunt?" she said. "I'll give you twenty-four hours. Get out of America, or I will make sure every fucking screen in the world has a picture of your face on it. You'll finally be notorious, just as you've always wanted. And then you'll be dead."

Lindy hung up the phone and detached the battery again. When she looked over, she saw Alex and Hadley staring at her. Hadley's eyes were very wide. She didn't look in any particular danger of falling asleep now. "What?" Lindy asked. Wasn't that pretty much what they'd discussed?

Alex cleared his throat. "You, um, you just sounded kind of scary at the end there."

"Oh. Sorry." She looked at both of them. "Listen ... just to be on the safe side, I think you should call your family, any close friends. Say whatever you have to say, just get them to take an overnight trip."

Hadley and Alex looked at each other for a second, then Alex turned back to Lindy with a little shrug. "Everyone I care about is already in this room," he said.

Hadley was looking down at one of the new burner phones. "My parents should be fine; they're in Palm

Springs. But can I . . ." She trailed off for a moment, then started again, more sure of herself. "Can I bring Faraday in on this?"

Lindy tried to hide her smile. Hadley had gone to high school with the state cop, and reconnected only the night before. It was unlikely that Hector would know about their relationship, or be able to find out in time. This was a good thing—Faraday's recent involvement made it unlikely that Hector would have gotten to him. They could use another ally. "It's fine with me," she said.

Alex added, "Have him meet us near the shoreline around four, and make sure he doesn't bring electronics, okay?"

"Okay. Should I wake up Ruiz and Eddy, so they can call their families too?"

"Don't worry about Chase," Alex answered. "His sister and parents are in Phoenix, but he got them out of town yesterday afternoon after he figured out that Hector's been mesmerizing him. They're safe."

Hadley nodded and stood up, stretching. "I'll tell Ruiz."

"Then get some rest," Alex called after her.

Lindy looked at him carefully. He needed to do the same, but she knew why he was stalling. "You should make the call," she said.

"I know." He sighed and picked up a burner phone.

Hadley had done some computer magic that would make it harder to pinpoint the call—not impossible, but harder. He dialed a number from heart and asked for the deputy director. It was Sunday morning, but she would have gone into the office after the first broadcast started.

The second he identified himself, he was put through—which was a really bad sign. "Alexander Michael McKenna!" Harding shouted over the phone. "What the *hell* do you think you're doing?"

Chapter 21

ALEX WINCED, pulling the phone away from his ear for a second. Ordinarily he'd be annoyed that she was talking to him like a mother chastising a child, even if she had *babysat* him back when his mother ran the Bureau. But under the circumstances, he'd let her have that one.

"Good morning, Deputy Director. I take it you saw the broadcast."

"Is it true? Is she really the queen of vampires?"

"It's true," he said. "And it's also true that she had nothing to do with Hector killing Tymer and the others."

There was a pause. When Harding came back on the line, she was speaking quietly. "Is she with you now?"

He glanced at Lindy, who was listening to the whole conversation. "Yes."

"Alex, I believe she may be mesmerizing you. Can you get away from her?"

Lindy raised an eyebrow, slightly amused. "If I wanted to," Alex said. "But she can't mesmerize me. Trust me on that."

"How can I?" Harding cried. "You went to the media,

Alex. We don't do that. We're the goddamned Bureau."

"We've used the media before to guide the direction of a case," Alex argued.

"With some idiot kidnapper in Kentucky, sure. But you just poked one of the oldest vampires on the planet with a stick. He's going to come after you."

"That's the idea," Alex said simply.

Her voice softened. "Where are you, Alex?"

"If I told you, what would you do?"

"Send help," she replied promptly.

Alex wavered for a second. Lindy's voice spoke in his head. *Do you trust her, that she'd just send help?*

He lifted his hand and tilted it back and forth. Harding might send help, but she also might just have him and Lindy both arrested. "I'm sorry, Marcia," Alex said quietly. He hadn't used her first name in over a decade. "But listen, if you want to go on TV and publicly renounce me as a renegade agent . . . would you mind waiting until tomorrow?"

There was a heavy sigh. "Oh, Alex." He waited, and more than thirty seconds ticked by.

"All right," she said, sounding tired. "Tell me your plan."

~

Alex ran her through most of the last two days, leaving out only sleeping with Lindy, the escape from her brownstone, and Chase's unwilling involvement with Hector. With Lindy's permission, Alex also told Harding more about Lindy and Hector's relationship and background.

In the end, the deputy director reluctantly agreed to let them go ahead with the plan. For now, the FBI's press office would be vague about the Bureau's reaction to the interview—but she warned Alex that if any more lives were lost, she would deny knowing about his actions in advance.

"But Alex, even if you get Hector, your little stunt this morning has changed the landscape," she added. "Ms. Frederick is going to have to go through with her promise to work with Congress, and become the public face of shades in the US. Is she up for that?"

Alex glanced at Lindy, who looked a little guilty. She was pawning off what was ultimately her own responsibility on Reagan, who was young and untested.

I'll help her, Lindy said in his head. *If we really do get Hector, we'll figure out how to make this work.*

Alex nodded and reached across the table to squeeze her hand. Into the phone, he said, "Let's do this one step at a time, Deputy Director."

"Fine." Alex recognized her tone: she was getting fed up with him. "I can't publicly back you—unless, of course, your operation is successful," she said wryly. "But behind the scenes . . . what can I do?"

"Keep the Coast Guard away from the Byrne water crib tonight," Alex said immediately.

Another heavy sigh. This might be a new record, even for him. "I can do that."

"And, um . . . maybe don't look too closely at the actions of some colleagues at the Chicago FBI this weekend," Alex suggested. "One or two of them may have given us a hand with some details."

After he hung up, Alex couldn't help but release a huge yawn. "You should get a few hours of sleep," Lindy said, looking anxious. "I'll keep an eye on things here." They both knew it was unlikely for Hector to be in Chicago already, and equally unlikely that he'd find them at the cabins, at least not so quickly.

"Yeah, you're right," he said, rubbing his eyes with the heel of his hand. Before he got up from the table, however, he glanced over his shoulder at the far end of the room. Ruiz had made whatever phone calls he needed to, and now he, Hadley, and Chase were all passed out on portable cots. They looked like they were at summer camp.

Two additional cots were already set up, currently

empty. Alex yearned to sleep, but there was something bothering him. He turned back to Lindy. "Do you mind if I ask you something personal?"

You've seen me naked. Aren't we kind of past that? But out loud, Lindy said, "You want to know why I don't want to be the queen of shades."

"Well, yeah. Don't get me wrong, I think Reagan can do a great job," he rushed to add. "But . . . not as good as you. You're stronger, smarter, and centuries more experienced. So why send her?"

"Because she wants it," Lindy said simply, but almost immediately she added, "Oh, it's more complicated than that, of course. Ultimately, it's probably just selfishness on my part. I've been hiding from Hector for a long time, and before that, I was his reluctant accomplice. I've spent lifetimes as a witness to such terrible things—from humans *and* shades." She gave him a sad smile. "Reagan is young and idealistic and hopeful. I haven't been those things for a long time."

Alex glanced at the others again to make sure they were sleeping, then he reached across the small table and took Lindy's hand, tugging her up and gently pulling her hand so she came around the table. When he put his arms around her, she climbed into his lap, wrapping her arms around him and leaning forward to rest on his shoulders.

Alex found himself marveling that he was even allowed to touch her.

Part of him had been worried that she was sending Reagan because of him. *Arrogant,* he thought now. But he didn't want to be the reason the world lost Lindy as their leader. "Lie down with me," he murmured into her hair.

Alex . . .

"I know. Just . . . lie down with me."

So she did.

Chapter 22

GIL PALMER SNAPPED THE rifle grip back into place and checked the cartridges one last time. Well, it wasn't actually called a rifle, but he refused to use Noelle's preferred term: Franken-gun. It looked like a rifle and fired much like a rifle, so he was going to think of it as a rifle, dammit. He needed a kite string back to reality, given how weird this whole situation was.

At two o'clock that morning, shortly after Liz Bassett and her charge had left the lab, a British shade named Sloane had presented himself at the office door and said that he was the evening's designated pincushion. Noelle had been delighted. After making sure that a little injected saline wouldn't hurt him, she had spent the next two hours shooting Sloane with her dart guns, making adjustments each time. The darts must have hurt, but Sloane never complained, only wincing a little in a stiff-upper-lip, British kind of way. After the first half-hour, he began actively trying to evade her, and by the time she was done, Noelle could pull the trigger before he could move out of the way. Sloane warned her that Hector was faster, but Noelle was satisfied that the rifle was as good as it was going to get.

Later, around four thirty, Sloane had unenthusiastically agreed to let Noelle try the methamphetamine on him. They had taken precautions first: she called Alex and warned him, Palmer drew his own weapon, and Noelle lit a small handheld propane torch and placed it on the table right next to her, in case Sloane attacked. She had been tinkering with the dose and formula on and off all night, and yet she seemed completely shocked when the methamphetamine injection did exactly what it was meant to do: after the dart hit, Sloane blinked, wobbled forward for two slow steps, and collapsed.

Noelle started to rush over to him, but Palmer made her wait, having her stand back with the propane torch until he could fasten a number of zip ties around Sloane's wrists, just in case. When he was positive Sloane couldn't break free, Palmer let Noelle come forward to take his temperature and check his vitals. He had none.

"Is he . . . *dead*-dead?" Palmer asked.

"I don't think so," she said, not sounding entirely certain. "Start the timer."

Palmer wasn't actually a lab assistant, but he had

learned by now that there was no point in reminding Noelle of this. He started a timer on his phone. Noelle, meanwhile, set about teaching him how to modify the dart guns.

It was delicate work, and Palmer was fully absorbed when, two hours and forty-five minutes later, Sloane began to twitch.

"Hey, kid!" Palmer yelled, and Noelle came racing from behind her desk.

Sloane sat up with a gasp. "Interesting," said Noelle.

"What?" Palmer asked.

"He doesn't need to breath as often as we do, but his body needs to pump oxygen in order to recover from the meth," she explained.

Sloane, meanwhile, had found his voice. "Bloody fucking hell," he gasped, still taking in big lungfuls of air. "And humans *like* this stuff?"

Noelle grinned at him. "You'd be surprised how much. Are you in pain?"

"No, not really, just feel a bit wonky. And also like I just rose from the dead. What time is it?"

"A little after seven," said Noelle.

"Bollocks. I've got to go meet Lindy and Reagan." He looked down at his arms. "Can we get these off now?"

After Sloane left, they had focused their energy on their weapons. Just before lunch—which they'd ordered in, like all the other food he'd eaten for the last day—Palmer had received a phone call from Deputy Director Harding on her personal cell phone, telling him to help McKenna however he could—but to keep it quiet. She explained a little bit of Alex's plan to stop Hector, and he made a decision: he was going with them. Palmer had lost six of his men on the first attempt to apprehend Hector; he wasn't about to miss the chance for a round two. Harding had told him to keep it quiet, so he wouldn't bring in the rest of his team, but . . . yeah. There was no way he was staying home. So he reconfigured the guns while Noelle did the fussy work of loading the darts with the right dosages.

Now it was almost four p.m., roughly two hours until sunset, and they were nearly finished. Noelle wanted a rifle and a sidearm for each person going to the water crib: Alex, Chase Eddy, Hadley, Ruiz, Sloane, Reagan, and Lindy. She didn't know that Lindy had turned down using a gun . . . because Palmer hadn't told her. He was planning to use those weapons himself.

By four thirty, Palmer had packed all but one rifle and one sidearm into massive ballistic duffel bags, borrowed from the weapons vault. He'd carry the rifle and sidearm when he went to meet the team at the harbor. "You have everything you need?" Noelle said, rubbing tiredly at her forehead. Palmer had caught a few hours of sleep during the research process, but she had been up and working for over forty-eight hours now. She looked more than ready to crash.

Palmer checked his watch. They were meeting at the harbor at 5:15, but he felt grimy and disgusting from the last two days. "Actually, do you mind if I grab a quick shower before I go?" The men's room down the hall had a shower stall, presumably for when the engineers worked late.

Noelle waved him on. "There are some towels in the cupboard by the door, there. They're not exactly five-star hotel quality, but they'll work."

"Thanks."

∼

In the washroom, Palmer locked the door, took off his gun belt, and climbed into the spray of hot water. He immediately felt revived, like he'd gotten a four-hour nap. Palmer wasn't a fastidious man, but in his early forties, he considered himself too old to disregard the small pleasures of being clean. Besides, he'd be confined in small spaces with the BPI pod. This was for their benefit too.

Ten minutes later, Palmer stepped out of the stall and dried himself off with two of Noelle's threadbare lab towels. He wished he'd brought some clean clothes along, but the gear in his car was what he'd worn to the raid on Lindy's brownstone the day before. At least he'd only worn this outfit to hang out in a climate-controlled building.

He had just started buttoning his shirt when he heard a crash from down the hall.

Chapter 23

PALMER FROZE, LISTENING. There were a couple of other technicians and lab assistants in the building today—he'd seen them on the way to and from the washroom—but that had sounded like it came directly from Noelle's lab.

Ignoring his socks and shoes, Palmer picked up his Glock and slowly unlocked the washroom door, hoping he was being paranoid. Noelle was exhausted; it would be totally understandable for her to knock something off a shelf. Still, he padded silently down the hall to the open lab door—and heard Noelle's scared voice.

"Stay back," she warned.

A male voice scoffed at her. "What are you, a lion tamer? Put it down, and this won't even hurt. It'll be just like going to sleep, I promise."

Palmer inched his back along the wall until he was right next to the doorframe. The voices were coming from inside the door and to the left, near the desk, but just then there was another small crash from the right.

At least two of them.

The same male voice laughed. "Jesus, she's jumpy. Come here, Wes. We don't have time for this shit."

Palmer risked peeking into the room. One man had backed Noelle into the far corner, behind her desk. She was holding a lab stool to her stomach—yes, like a lion tamer, but it was smart. If he couldn't touch her, he couldn't mesmerize her. If he mesmerized her, it was over.

But the second man had just run past the doorway in a near-blur. Shades. Two shades.

There were three leftover syringes on Noelle's desk, but she'd have to drop the stool to get them. Palmer's modified sidearm was two tables inside the door and three tables over; he'd never reach it in time.

But he had his service weapon.

Palmer stepped into the room. "FBI!" he yelled. "Stop right there!"

The man closest to Noelle sniggered, and Palmer realized that he recognized his face. This was Ambrose, the shade who had spent over a year imprisoned at Camp Vamp. Before he'd helped kill a bunch of BPI agents in order to escape.

The second shade—Wes—had stopped on the other side of the desk from Noelle. He'd obviously been just about to jump over it and come at her sideways, but now he looked to Ambrose for directions.

The famous vampire sneered at Palmer. "What are you, behind? Bullets won't—"

Palmer squeezed the trigger, over and over.

He was pretty sure the first one had been a solid chest shot, but after that, Ambrose was moving toward him in a blur. After five shots Palmer stopped firing, because Ambrose was moving too fast to aim. He was suddenly in front of Palmer, clubbing him carelessly along the side of his head.

Palmer went down hard, losing the gun. His head hit the floor.

"Hang on a minute, Wes," Ambrose called over his shoulder. There was a gunshot wound on his chest, and another had grazed his forearm, but Ambrose paid as much attention to them as Palmer would to a mosquito bite. Instead, Ambrose looked down at Palmer in his bare feet and unbuttoned shirt. "What the hell is going on here? I know you two aren't banging. Our intel is that she's a dyke."

He stepped toward the table nearest the door, the one with the duffel bags. Palmer sat up, but Ambrose just raised a finger at him, warning him not to go for the gun. "Wes can rip out her throat before you get your finger around the trigger," he warned. He unzipped the bag and peeked inside, letting out a low whistle. "I see. Well. This is an unexpected bonus." He looked at Palmer and shook his head almost sadly. "You guys are behind the times, huh? Hector had weapons like this *years* ago."

"Not like this," Noelle said through gritted teeth. She was pointing the stool at Wes now, but glaring at Ambrose. *Good for you,* Palmer thought.

"Wes, do it," Ambrose said in a bored voice. He was still studying the bag. Palmer started to inch toward his gun, but Ambrose bared his teeth at the FBI agent. "*Stay down.*"

Wes slapped the stool away and climbed over the desk before she could react. His head darted forward and he slid his tongue up her cheek. "Ew!" Noelle cried, but her eyes were already glazing over.

Ambrose smirked, watching her. He waited two heartbeats, then asked Noelle, "Where is the woman who calls herself Rosalind Frederick?"

"I don't know."

Palmer had seen and done a lot in his career, but the sound of Noelle's empty, lifeless voice hurt his heart. "Track that bracelet she wears," Ambrose ordered.

Without another word, Noelle opened the laptop on her desk, bent at the waist, and began typing. "Don't do it, kid!" Palmer yelled. Ambrose took three steps toward him and kicked him hard in the side of the head, right where he'd hit Palmer before. Palmer fell sideways with a groan, seeing actually bursts of stars, but the shade kicked him again for good measure. This time he got Palmer in the stomach, and the FBI agent doubled over into the fetal position, fighting not to vomit. He lost the battle, and threw up in a puddle.

Ambrose wrinkled his nose in disgust, backing away a few steps. "*This* is the best and brightest the FBI can offer?" he scoffed. "An over-the-hill bodyguard and a computer dyke?"

"She's at Montrose Harbor," Noelle said, in the same empty tone.

"Excellent." Ambrose looked at the other shade and said, "Wes, text Hector." To Noelle, he added, "How do I get there?"

As soon as they knew exactly where to go to find Lindy, the shades would have no reason to keep either of them alive. "Noelle," Palmer gasped. "You have to wake up. You have to run."

Ambrose chuckled, turning his attention to Palmer. "Do you know how many times I had to eat shit from you FBI guys when I was in that cell?" he said. "You assholes act so tough, but look at you. You're just a pathetic skin bag like the rest of them. So *breakable*." He stomped down on Palmer's forearm, which made an audible snapping sound. Palmer cried out.

"See?" Ambrose said, as though he'd just made a complicated point.

"You . . . got what you wanted," Palmer managed to say. "Just go. Security will have heard the shots."

"*Security?*" Ambrose sounded incredulous, and Palmer's last hope of rescue sank. The shade squatted down in front of Palmer. "You don't think we ate everyone in this building before we came here? How do you think we found the right office? How do you think I healed from bullet wounds so fast? I thought you were supposed to be like a detective." He rolled his eyes, and a little chime sound came from the phone Wes was holding. Ambrose turned to look over his shoulder. "What's he say?"

"Kill 'em and come back."

"All right. Fun time is—"

But while Ambrose had looked away the FBI agent lifted a leg and braced himself. Now he stomp-kicked Ambrose right in the balls. He felt a very gross—and very satisfying—*squish*.

As it turned out, shades were still pretty sensitive there.

Ambrose let out a grunt and toppled sideways, his face frozen in pain and surprise. A human would have passed out from the pain, but he just made some strangled noises, and Palmer knew he only had seconds. He rolled over and started elbow-crawling toward his gun.

Wes, who hadn't seen what had happened because of

the tables, called, "Ambrose?"

"Noelle!" Palmer screamed, but there was no answer. Ambrose was already moving, starting to crawl after him with a look of intense, furious hatred.

Palmer cleared the last row of tables and picked up the Glock. He had a clear shot at either Ambrose or Wes, but it wasn't going to be enough. They were too fast, too powerful. He felt a wave of despair, and a shameful thought flickered through his head: *Turn the gun on yourself.* But he could never do that to Noelle.

Noelle. Palmer had read all the reports from the Switch River case, and the cop who'd been shot, Amanda something, had said that she and the other cops who'd been mesmerized had been able to wake themselves up when they heard gunshots. They'd all spent years and years training to react to the sound of shots, and it had worked like an alarm clock.

Palmer took shaky aim and fired at Ambrose. He hit the shade in the top of the shoulder—but it didn't seem to affect Noelle, who was still staring lifelessly at the screen. Ambrose snarled, a purely predator sound.

"Ambrose?" Wes called. He had started to move away from Noelle.

"Kill her!" Ambrose yelled.

Wes turned around again—and Palmer put a bullet in the back of his kneecap, causing the shade to buckle sideways with a howl. It bought him seconds. "Come on, Noelle!" he yelled again.

And then Palmer had his best, and last, idea. He raised the gun again, took the time to aim carefully, and fired a perfect shot, right through the meat of Noelle's upper arm. The engineer yelped, clutching her arm and looking around the room in confusion. *Oh, thank God.*

"The syringes!" Palmer yelled, but now he had to turn his attention to Ambrose, whose eyes were fully red now. He'd already healed all his injuries, which just didn't seem *fair*—so Palmer shot him through the right eye. Or he tried to, anyway—the bullet made a small hole in Ambrose's cheek, and the shade got the strangest look of confusion on his face. He snarled one more time and darted toward Palmer like a lizard. Palmer tried to move away, but Ambrose grabbed his ankle, his thigh bone, both climbing Palmer's body and pulling it closer. Palmer clubbed at him with the gun, but Ambrose grabbed his broken forearm and Palmer screamed, his vision exploding into white nothingness.

Holding down the broken arm, Ambrose dragged himself across Palmer's body and bit down on the opposite wrist, his teeth tearing and worrying at the veins, breaking through the delicate bones there. Palmer could do nothing but watch, as his vision regrettably returned to him.

Behind Ambrose, Palmer saw Wes's body fall. Noelle stood over him with her syringe, panting. Ambrose must have heard the sound, because he jerked away from Palmer's wrist and turned to see Noelle advancing with the other syringe and absolute murder in her eyes.

Ambrose growled like a wild thing, but he recognized the syringe. "How would you like a trip back to Camp Vamp, asshole?" Noelle snapped. "All expenses paid. Leaving tonight."

Palmer couldn't see Ambrose's face, but the shade flinched away from her, scrambling to his feet. He started to circle the tables toward the door, but Noelle advanced on him. Ambrose snarled, and Palmer didn't know if he'd attack or run. He struggled to stand, but both arms were useless now.

Ambrose backed toward Palmer, grabbing the FBI agent by the neck and lifting him bodily to his feet. Palmer thought he was going to pass out, but his eyes caught a shape on the table nearest him, and it was like a splash of water on his face.

"Let me pass," Ambrose snarled at Noelle. "Or I break his neck now."

Don't think about the pain, Palmer told himself. *Just do it.*

He reached out and grabbed the modified dart gun, the sidearm he'd been planning to take for himself, with his broken arm. Ambrose, who didn't look away from Noelle, must have thought he was just trying to wriggle free, because he didn't stop Palmer from scooping up the gun, screaming with pain. By the time Ambrose realized what was happening and released Palmer to grab for the dart gun, Palmer was able to shove his bloodied fingers in the trigger guard and shoot—

The dart hit Ambrose in the hand. Palmer crumpled to the floor, feeling things inside him give way. Important things.

Ambrose took one, two steps and collapsed. But Noelle wasn't taking any chances. She ran forward and buried the second syringe in Ambrose's chest, aiming straight for his heart.

She jumped up and ran for the door, closing and bolting it, then she raced back to Palmer, looking down at Ambrose's body on the way. "I think I killed him . . . Palmer? Gil! Holy shit, that's a lot of blood." Noelle began to move, holding a phone to her ear with a shoulder and babbling into it.

She was ripping up a lab towel at the same time, but Palmer knew how much blood he'd lost. His whole forearm was shredded, all those delicate little veins. "Noelle," he whispered.

"I'm so sorry." There were tears in her eyes as she pressed the towel over his forearm, but it didn't even hurt. He was going into shock. He tried to speak, and she bent her head close to hear him.

"Get the guns to Alex," Palmer whispered.

Noelle began to sob. "Gil, you can't die! You just can't! The ambulance is coming, it'll be here—"

"It's okay, kid. I'll be with Lori soon."

Noelle said something else, but he didn't hear her. Special Agent Gil Palmer let his eyes close. He'd protected Noelle, and the two of them had killed Ambrose. He hadn't gotten to go after Hector, but Alex and Lindy could do it. He could rest now.

He thought of his wife, and drifted away.

Chapter 24

PARKING LOT ON MONTROSE DRIVE
LATE SUNDAY AFTERNOON

MONTROSE HARBOR WAS NESTLED inside a slice of beach shaped roughly like a hook. Alex had seen satellite images online, and the harbor looked like the inside of a huge, sideways letter D, with a small opening in the bottom of the letter that led to Lake Michigan.

By mid-October, most of the boats had been winterized and put away, but he'd managed to find a couple of commercial fishermen who worked until early November and were willing to rent out their vessels for a hefty fee. He'd said he was a law enforcement officer doing a team-building competition. Both Sloane and Ruiz knew their way around boats and could pilot them out to the water crib. The boats—or was it ships? Alex new nothing about nautical terms—were old but sturdy, and he'd deliberately chosen them because the Bureau could afford to replace them if something happened.

He'd also made sure there were plenty of life vests.

Now Alex and the others were in the large parking lot just across the street from the harbor. It was long and slightly arched, completely empty except for their three vehicles. The harbor office closed early at this time of year.

Alex paced back and forth, checking his watch every few minutes and berating himself for cutting everything so close. He'd wanted his people to get a few hours of sleep before they went against Hector and his shades, and Noelle had needed time to finish what she'd called her Franken-guns, but now it was starting to get dark. Already he could barely see past the stadium-sized lights of the parking lot.

Hector couldn't know where they were, but still. Palmer was supposed to be here twenty minutes ago to deliver the guns. Alex had checked in with Noelle's lab several times during the day, and only an hour ago everything had been fine. It wasn't like the FBI agent to be late, and now he wasn't answering his cell. No one was answering the phone in Noelle's lab, either, and her phone went straight to voicemail. Alex had planned to be out on the water crib by now.

He stopped pacing long enough to zip up his windbreaker. Chicago had been enjoying a rare streak of warm fall sunshine, but the temperature had plummeted during the day. Now it was fifty-five degrees, windy, and misting in that obnoxious sideways manner, where you got wet even with an umbrella. They had managed to dig up baseball caps for everyone so the mist stayed out of their eyes, but everyone was still soaked and miserable.

In a way, though, the weather was good: the harbor was deserted, and the clouds were so thick that all three shades had an easier time being out in the daylight. Even Reagan, the youngest of them, seemed fine with being outside. She was now flushed and bright-eyed. Lindy had driven separately with the other two shades so they could make a stop to feed before facing Hector's people. All the humans had been a little uncomfortable about it, but Alex trusted Lindy to make sure no one were seriously hurt, and he couldn't have his own people making blood donations right now.

"What do we do if he doesn't show up?" Hadley asked, scratching at her neckline. At Alex's request, they were all wearing civilian clothes over their gear, so they wouldn't raise any red flags if they bumped into civilians at the harbor. She was sitting on the tailgate of Ruiz's pickup truck. Faraday stood next to her: a lean, handsome Asian American cop in jeans and a black windbreaker. He leaned slightly so he was just touching her leg. He was obviously nervous, and had been pretty quiet since his arrival.

"He'll show up," Alex said, trying to sound confident.

Lindy was watching him. *Should we send someone to the*

FBI building to check on them?

Alex shielded his eyes from the mist and looked across the street to the harbor and Lake Michigan, thinking it over. They only had eight people, and five were humans. They just couldn't afford to split their resources if Hector somehow figured out where they were. "We'll give him ten more minutes," Alex decided. "Hopefully they just fell behind on modifying the weapons." If Palmer didn't get there soon, he'd send half his people ahead to the water crib to start setting up the generator and electric lights. Shades could see easier in the darkness than humans could, and he didn't want the human members of the team to be at a disadvantage.

"How many people do you think he'll bring?" Faraday asked Lindy. The rest of them had discussed it on the way there.

"Enough to show us that he's powerful and well connected, but not so many that he seems like he's afraid of me," she said patiently. "I would guess five minimum, ten at the most."

Just then Gil's blue Camry careened into the lot, and Alex's shoulders slumped with relief. "That's him."

But it was immediately obvious that something was wrong. Alex couldn't see much through the misty, tinted windows, but as the car screeched to a stop a few feet away he noticed a big smear of red on the driver's handle.

It was still wet, and thick enough that the mist hadn't cleared it.

Alex put up a hand to stop the others and approached the door slowly, one hand on his sidearm. "Palmer?" he yelled.

The driver's door opened, and Noelle half-fell, half-staggered out. Reagan and Sloane immediately turned away, holding their breath. Even Lindy flinched, her jaw tightening.

Because Noelle was drenched in blood.

She was also weeping, and mascara had run down her face into the collar of her T-shirt. She didn't even have a jacket. Alex and Chase ran forward at the same moment. "Nell!" Chase cried, helping her to her feet. "What happened? Where are you hurt?"

"They—they killed Palmer," she sobbed. "It's his blood." She leaned into Chase as though she were no longer able to stay upright without help. He wrapped his arms around her.

"She's bleeding," Sloane remarked. He and Reagan had taken a couple of steps away. Lindy stayed where she was, but she looked distracted.

Noelle blinked in surprise. "Oh. My arm . . ."

Alex looked at Hadley, but she was already running for the new first aid kit they'd put in the SUV. "They came to the lab," Noelle said to Chase, half-babbling, "and-and-they made me use Lindy's bracelet to get your location. I don't know how they even knew about me; I'm not in the BPI . . ."

Over her shoulder, Alex and Chase exchanged a horrified look. Chase must have told Hector. Chase obviously hadn't realized this was part of Hector's questioning, because in that moment he looked like he'd been run over by a semi.

Hadley and Faraday started wrapping Noelle's arm with gauze, and Lindy opened the trunk of Gil's car, exposing a very heavy-looking bag inside. Alex went to help her, but she lifted it out like it was a package of toilet paper. "This is really bad," she said to him.

Her voice was low, but not low enough. "Of course this is bad!" Noelle practically screamed, turning to face Lindy. "They *killed* Palmer!"

"You don't understand." Lindy sounded calm, but she was unzipping the bag and hurriedly passing out weapons to a bewildered-looking Ruiz, Hadley, and Faraday. "How long ago was this?"

Noelle blinked, and Alex could see her trying to get it together. "Maybe forty minutes?"

Lindy checked her watch. "What is it?" Alex asked her.

"Sunset," she said grimly. "The sun sets in ten minutes. If they know where we are—"

"We need to get to the boats," Alex finished. "Okay,

everybody grab your—"

There was a quiet crack, and the overhead light on the far end of the parking lot flickered out. Everyone went still, and at the other end of the rectangular parking lot, there was another crack and another light disappeared. The next two cracks were almost simultaneous, and the next closest rows of lights were gone.

They were surrounded.

Chapter 25

THE HUMANS FROZE WITH shock, and Lindy knew this was the point: a dramatic darkening to scare everyone. Mind games. Classic Hector.

She yelled loud enough to break them out of it. "Hey!" Everyone looked over. "They'll have blocked the exits, they're gonna kill the lights," she said in as low a voice as would carry to them. "Faraday, Chase, you need to move the cars together *right now*. Make as much light as possible."

The two men nodded and immediately took off. They'd parked their vehicles a few rows away to be less conspicuous. Meanwhile, Lindy finished handing out the guns. There was one extra set, which she gave to Noelle. "Get in the Camry," she ordered, wishing they had a vehicle with bullet-resistant glass. "Reagan, stay with her and lock the doors." Noelle did as she said, but the younger shade began to protest. Lindy overrode her. "You promised if I let you come you would listen to me. Protect Noelle."

Reagan's mouth snapped shut. She looked unhappy,

but she climbed in after the human engineer. A second later the door cracked open and something dropped onto the pavement: Noelle's bloody shirt. Reagan didn't want it in the closed space, where it would force her to vamp out. Lindy approved.

Faraday pulled his Lexus sedan in line with the pickup, moving forward until the sedan's nose touched the truck's grill. Chase did the same with the rental SUV and the Camry, so there was a narrow corridor between the two sets of vehicles. All the drivers turned the headlights and interior lights on just as the last streetlights in the lot exploded into darkness.

The vehicles formed an oasis of light that looked ghostly in the mist. "Shit, shit, shit," Hadley was muttering, checking her rifle. "Five rounds each," she announced.

"There are more clips or magazines or whatever in the bottom of the bag," Lindy said absently. She was scanning the darkness.

Faraday and Chase were back, and everyone instinctively moved into the long aisle created by the cluster of cars.

"Run for the boats?" Alex said to Lindy. They'd have to cross the road, not to mention half a parking lot of open space, to get to it.

She shook her head. *We'd never make it.* But they had

to do something. Even with the cars as partial cover, they were in serious trouble. If Hector had a bunch of shades and they all decide to rush them at once . . .

"How do you want to play this?" Alex asked. He sounded calm, but she could hear his pulse racing, along with everyone else's.

Stay there. I'll see if I can Gordian knot this thing before it gets bad.

Without waiting for a response, Lindy climbed on top of the Camry. It was slippery from the rain, but she was wearing rubber-soled hiking boots and had a thousand years of supernatural balance behind her. She reached the roof and looked out into the darkness, though it was hard to see or smell anything through the misting rain. There were shapes moving at the edges of the lot, for sure.

Too many shapes. Way more than ten. Lindy didn't take the time to count, but she would estimate upward of thirty. Fuck, Hector had been recruiting. Probably just for this.

Alex, I think he turned enough new shades to make a herd. It's like the outbreak I told you about.

Without waiting for his reaction, she opened her arms wide. "Hector!" she shouted, legitimately furious. "Are you so afraid to face me that you resort to stupid theatrics?"

There was no answer. Then a distinctive *pop* broke the

silence, followed by a little whistling sound, and Lindy took a dart right in the chest.

She looked down and saw one of Hector's little methamphetamine vials. Goddammit.

Lindy jumped down from the Camry, landing in the middle of their safe zone—okay, it wasn't actually *safe*, but it was the only cover they were likely to get. She plucked the dart from the top layer of Kevlar and tossed it to the ground.

"You okay?" Alex called. Lindy nodded. She, Sloane, and Reagan were all wearing three layers of bulletproof vests—another one of Noelle's ideas. The theory was that the Kevlar would slow down the needle, which wouldn't be able to embed itself properly, and the methamphetamine liquid would release harmlessly between the vests. Good to see it worked.

"Boss!" Hadley screamed. She and Faraday were positioned at one end of the corridor. "They're coming!"

Faraday and Hadley both fired, but Lindy knew her brother well enough to whirl around and race for the other end, pulling the push daggers from underneath the bottom of her vests. Ruiz and Chase, who were stationed at this gap, saw her coming and instinctively flattened themselves against the cars, which is how they avoided the shade diving toward them. Lindy clashed straight into the stranger—a female—and their opposing momentums made them land just past the edge of the cars.

"I didn't even see her!" Lindy heard Chase exclaim, but Lindy was already using one push dagger to slice across the girl's throat and one to disembowel her.

"Jesus," Ruiz said from only a few feet away. The female let out a gurgling snarl and swiped at Lindy's midsection with a short sword. Lindy ducked back, pulling her blades free, and the female struggled to get up. She was too weak to heal fast enough, and Lindy felt a swell of pity. This one was even younger than Reagan.

Chase shot her in the arm with the dart gun. The female blinked a few times, and then all her muscles relaxed as the meth took her.

There was a lot of shooting at the other end, and then Chase and Ruiz were yelling back and forth over the gunfire. When the next shade attempted to leap over the cars and land in between them, Chase was aiming low while Ruiz was aiming high. She felt a jolt of relief. Ruiz had seen shade attacks before, he had known they would jump.

Then Lindy couldn't keep an eye on them any longer, because of course the young female was just the first. The next shade was already barreling toward her through the dark rain.

He was bigger, and older, and Lindy could hear actual chain mail clicking from his neck down into his pants.

Hector knew what weapons she favored. Lindy tried to swipe a blade just below his jaw line, but the man dodged, bringing up a gun that Lindy easily kicked out of his hand. He grunted in annoyance and reached into his back belt, coming out with a brutal-looking knife that had been welded to a set of brass knuckles so it couldn't easily be knocked away.

Lindy put her best "scared little girl" expression on her face and took an uncertain step backward. *Alex. Get ready to shoot this guy in the face when I duck.* The chain mail guy grinned and advanced on her, past the edges of the car and into the safe zone. He swiped the knife at her neck, and Lindy threw herself to the pavement like she was starting a backflip. From the other end of their base, Alex's rifle fired, and the dart hit the chain mail guy in the cheek almost the moment Lindy heard the sound. *Holy shit. Noelle was good.*

Then there were no more shades coming toward her end of the safe zone, which alarmed her. Lindy took one second to stop and look around. At the other end, Faraday and Hadley seemed to have fallen into a good rhythm of alternating shooting and reloading as shades ran toward them in groups of two or three. Chase, Ruiz, and Alex were protecting both sides, where the cars touched. But where was Sloane? Lindy looked toward the Camry, of course—he wouldn't go far from Reagan during a fight. She spotted him on the other side of the Camry, fighting two shades who had succeeded in breaking one of the car's windows. Sloane seemed to be holding his own, though, using an actual sword. He hadn't had that before—must have taken it off someone.

Lindy wished she could talk into *their* heads.

Behind her, Alex cried out, and she whirled around to see a slender male shade, this one also with chain mail, pushing a blade deep into the muscle of Alex's shoulder as Alex struggled to get his sidearm up. Lindy was instantly there with her blades, scissoring them against the back of the guy's neck, severing his spinal cord. His head flopped forward, and she kicked the body aside.

Alex looked pale, and he wasn't lifting that arm. She bent forward and kissed him, hoping the shot of saliva would be enough. She broke the contact only to snap an arm out and slice the throat of the next approaching shade, a male that Alex shot with his dart gun. "Thanks," he panted. He glanced around too. "We can't hold them off for long, not like this."

She had to turn to bat aside a running shade, taking two more darts in her vest, but in his head she said, *I know. There are too many of them.* This was her fault—she had counted on Hector's arrogance, his pride. She should have remembered his desire for an army.

And that's what they were. As she glanced toward

Hadley and Faraday, she could see that the shades were coordinating, running toward the side that was most vulnerable—the one with the humans.

Hector was directing all of them. Lindy had never had more than four or five different fledglings at one time, because it had been hard to keep them straight in her head. Now Hector was trying to direct all these minds at once? No wonder he was crazy.

Still, in order to control these people he had to have a better vantage point. Somewhere high.

She kissed Alex again, a quick peck. "Hold them off, I'm going after Hector."

He protested, of course, but the sun had set, and she was long gone before he finished the words.

Chapter 26

THERE WAS REALLY ONLY one place high enough to see everything: the corner of the harbor building across the street. It was a little far even for shade eyesight, but the headlights would be spotlighting a relatively small amount of space, like being in the balcony of a theatrical performance. It was probably giving Hector quite a thrill.

Lindy ran through the encroaching shades like a bowling ball through pins, doing as much quick damage as she could with her push daggers and a few kicks. She sped across the street, holstered her blades, and leapt on top of the shed right next to the building. A few running steps and she jumped for the building, punching her hands into the siding to pull herself up.

Hector was right where she'd expected, peering over the building's edge with great concentration.

Lindy paused. This seemed too easy.

"You left them vulnerable," Hector called without turning around. His voice was strained, his concentration divided. "I wasn't sure you would."

Lindy ignored the comment and barreled toward her

brother, who spun around with a dart gun in hand. Lindy ducked it—his weapons *were* slower than Noelle's—and tackled him at the waist. He went down with a strangled cry.

And then he hit her, a perfect punch to her face that shattered her cheekbone and cracked her jaw.

It had been a *long* time since Lindy had fought someone as old or as strong as her, and Hector was both. She had healed many injuries, but a shattered bone was probably the worst. The fragments of her cheekbone immediately began trying to knit together, which was excruciating.

It was also distracting, which had been his plan. He stood up. "Oh, Lindy," he sighed. "When will you learn that hitting things isn't the answer?"

Probably when you stop being so hittable, she thought, but it hurt too much to speak just yet. She snaked out a leg and toppled him, reaching for one of her push daggers. They grappled for a moment, but Lindy got his arm locked behind his back. "Call them off," she said through her teeth, trying to ignore the pain. "Now."

His eyes filled with glee. "That's your plan? Torture me until I stop picking on your little human friends? Come on, Sieglinde. You're the next best thing to a goddess. Surely you can aim higher than fucking some government drone."

Lindy sliced across his throat, just to get his attention. Blood sprayed, and he couldn't speak for a moment while it healed, which in itself was a relief.

She used the quiet time to repeat herself, ignoring the pain in her face. "Call. Them. Off."

Hector winced, and when he could speak, he said, "As you wish, sister."

That brought her up short, as she realized she couldn't stand up and check for herself without letting go of him. Hector saw her predicament and laughed.

"Don't worry," he assured her. "You'll know in a moment. They're all on their way here."

~

Back in the safe zone, Alex McKenna had run out of methamphetamine darts and was hitting a shade with the butt of his rifle, trying to get her to release Chase's arm from her teeth. He pounded on her forehead, but she seemed to only bite down harder. "Somebody shoot her!" he screamed.

Faraday spun around to shoot, but at that exact moment the female shade simply released Chase, who fell back against Alex. The parking lot was slippery with rain, and the two men went down in a tangle. By the time Alex disengaged and stood up, the first thing he saw was Ruiz, standing still, looking confused. There was no one attacking him.

Alex glanced to the other end, where Hadley was tying a tourniquet around Faraday's lower leg. "One of them crawled under the cars," she called by way of explanation. "What's happening? Why'd they stop?"

"I don't—" he began, but then Alex *did* know.

The massive vampire attack hadn't been for him or his people. Hector didn't really give a shit about a handful of humans. All he cared about was revenge on his sister.

This whole thing had been a trap for *her*.

"Get your stuff!" he shouted. "Lindy went after Hector; they're going to kill her!"

Ruiz and Hadley looked scuffed and breathless, but unharmed. They reloaded their guns and trotted toward Alex. Chase started to move toward him too, but Alex held up a hand. The bite wound looked bad. Alex didn't think any major arteries had been severed, but he could still bleed out without medical attention. "Faraday, get him a tourniquet too!" he called, and the state cop nodded and motioned for Chase to come over.

"Sloane!"

"Right here, boss!" The British shade seemed to suddenly materialize at Alex's elbow. "I need eyes on that roof," Alex said, pointing. It was the only possible vantage point for Hector. "Can you go up and come down without getting killed?"

Sloane's teeth flashed. "You know in horror movies, how one of the humans covers himself in gore and sneaks by the zombies?"

"Just go!"

Sloane vanished, and Alex went to check on Noelle and Reagan. Three windows and the windshield had been shattered on the Camry, but they looked unharmed. He wasn't sure the car would run, so he called for Ruiz's keys and tossed them to Reagan. "Get her out of here while you can," he ordered.

The two women started to climb out, but Reagan handed the keys to Noelle. To Alex, she simply said, "I promised I would listen to Lindy. I didn't say anything about you." Then she followed Sloane toward the building, disappearing instantly.

Alex cursed and looked at Noelle. "Can you drive yourself out of here?"

She nodded. "Should I call the police?"

Alex hesitated. If he brought in more humans, would he doing any good, or just setting up a buffet?

Luckily, Faraday answered for him. "I'm calling the state cops from my department," he announced, already pulling out a cell phone. "We'll start securing these prisoners."

Alex nodded a thank you and looked back at Noelle.

"Call—" He paused, and realized he'd been about to say Gil. But Gil was dead. "Whoever else you can at the Bureau," he said instead. "Get some of them here to help the state cops, and the rest to your building to start processing the scene. Jessica Reyes, the coroner, knows about shade violence; she should be there."

Noelle nodded, and as Alex and his team finished gathering weapons, she started the pickup, bumped her way over a number of bodies, and pulled onto the street.

Sloane reappeared. "You guys better get up here," he said breathlessly. "No joke. She needs help."

"Go help her then!" Alex yelled.

"We're trying! Hector keeps sending them at us!" Sloane turned and vanished again.

Alex looked at Hadley and Ruiz, wanting to give them an out. "I know this is really stupid—"

"But we're gonna do it anyway," Hadley interrupted. "We know. Let's go, boss."

Chapter 27

LINDY WAS BEING SWARMED.

Hector must have ordered them all to attack at once, and now shades were climbing over the side of the roof like ants to a picnic—if ants were super-fast, crazed, and armed.

At first she was okay, ducking and slashing and kicking out, but then Hector climbed onto the roof's ledge so he could direct them like an orchestra. She took about six darts in the vest, dodging a couple that nearly hit her face. One of them swung an actual ax at her, and she had to throw herself sideways to avoid being dismembered. Lindy rolled to her feet and gritted her teeth with anger, which hurt her still-knitting cheekbone. She had come to fight Hector, and he was using over a dozen shades as his weapon of choice. Typical.

If she'd fed more, and more recently, it would have been easier, but once they started to crowd her, she knew she was running on borrowed time. A female successfully wrenched a push dagger from one of her hands, and Lindy felt real fear. She couldn't even get the breathing room to form a strategy; she was just reacting. And she was going to lose.

Hector was on the edge of the roof.

Lindy did the only possible thing she could think of: she ran straight across the roof, as fast as she could, which surprised the attackers enough to keep them from stopping her. Hector, who had been concentrating on coordinating the entire outbreak, didn't have time to react before she tackled him around the waist, hurling both of them off the roof.

Down, down they fell, each trying to position themselves to brace for landing. In films people could have whole fights while they fall, but the laws of aerodynamics just didn't work like that. With great effort, Lindy managed to get her legs under her, landing in a half-crouch that cracked one ankle and the opposite kneecap.

Hector hadn't fared as well: he'd landed on his back ten feet away, and she could tell by the way he went still that he'd snapped some vertebrae. He was still conscious, though, and staring straight up, his face was filled with terrible wrath.

She knew that expression. He was ready to burn it all down.

He could do anything: send his people after the BPI team, or the people of Chicago in general. Maybe he would order them to kill each other. At this moment, there really wasn't anything that Hector wasn't capable of.

Lindy needed to stop him *now*. She tried to stand up and succeeded only in toppling forward onto her hands and one good knee. She began dragging herself toward him, but all the required healing had weakened her. She wasn't sure she could snap his neck again before Hector could heal himself. And if he got away again . . .

Alex, we're back on the ground, northwest corner of the building. I need a dart now.

~

The order came into all their heads, every shade who'd been made by Hector, at the same time, in the same words.

Kill the BPI humans. Tear them apart.

It was a really, really unfortunate moment for Hadley, Alex, and Ruiz to burst through the roof doors.

Immediately, the shades closest to the door bared their teeth, tensing to spring. Ruiz, who was in the front, almost pissed himself.

And then a young blond woman in an army jacket

stepped in front of him, between him and the mob. "Everybody *stop*," she screamed, so loudly that Ruiz half-expected glass to shatter, like in a cartoon.

But it worked: the dozen or so vampires in front of her all froze with a look of confusion. Reagan was young, yes, but they were younger still.

"You don't have to listen to him," she said in a quieter voice. "I know he made you think you have to take orders. I know it feels good, it feels *right,* to obey him. He's probably convinced you that you don't have a choice. But you *do not have to listen to him*."

For the first time, the shades seemed to pause and look at each other. "Who are you?" said a female shade near the front. She looked about forty, and wore a cardigan and high-waisted jeans.

Reagan took a breath. "My name is Reagan," she answered. "And I used to be just like you."

This seemed to confuse the other shades even further, but at least they'd stopped attacking. Ruiz glanced over his shoulder at Alex for new instructions—but Alex wasn't there. He could hear feet pounding back the way they'd come.

What the hell?

~

Alex raced down the stairs, barely managing not to tumble down them headfirst. He didn't know the building's interior, but Hadley had broken a windowpane to get them in a side door, and he retraced the route with terror driving his limbs faster than he thought possible. His fear for Lindy was foremost, but a voice in his head, the cop voice, was also screaming that Hector *couldn't* get away now, not after all this.

Panting, Alex burst through the outer door and ran around the corner—where he saw the strangest scene. Lindy was sitting on the pavement next to her brother, who was lying on his back, his arms and legs twitching in tiny, restless movements. Alex couldn't hear what he was saying to her, but the look of terrible sorrow on her face physically hurt him.

Then he heard the sirens.

It was so odd: Lindy had spent all this time hating and chasing Hector, even trying to kill him, but in this quiet moment, her heart was just glad to see her twin brother. She wanted to lie down next to him and stare up at the sky, which had finally stopped spitting out rain. Being in Hector's presence, not fighting him, felt so wrong . . . and at the same time completely natural.

"Come with me, then," Hector was saying. "How long do you think you can play human? How long before they decide you're too big of a threat to run free?"

"It's not like that," she protested, her voice coming out so much younger- and weaker-sounding than she'd wanted. "Alex isn't like that."

"Ah yes, *Alex*. You know if I go to Camp Vamp, I can still give orders. I can do anything, get to anyone. You'll always be looking over your shoulder for the ones I send."

Lindy tried to get hold of herself. "I could kill you," she said. "Pretty much solve all my problems."

"Could you?" Hector's eyes were little-boy-huge. "I know you're a killer, Lindy. But I'm the last person on the planet who knows you, who knows all of you. Even the dark parts. Could you really kill me?"

Lindy heard the sirens, then, and noticed Alex in her peripheral vision. He was sidling toward her.

"I know everything you've done, and I love you anyway," Hector went on. "I'm the only one."

Is that true?

She hadn't realized she'd pushed the thought out until she heard Alex reply.

"Of course not, dummy," he said. Lindy struggled to sit up so she could see him. Alex had stopped a few feet away, and when she looked over he grinned at her and tossed something small and shiny in her direction. Lindy caught the dart gun and turned it on her brother.

"Lindy, no—" Hector began. She tried to think of something to say, but what? She wasn't sorry. She didn't regret this. "Don't—"

She pulled the trigger.

Unlike the other, younger shades, it took a moment for Hector's eyes to begin to lose focus. "Remember the wheat?" he whispered.

She did: the two of them, age ten or eleven, spinning in endless circles in a field of tall wheat, letting the plants catch them as they fell over. They'd gotten in trouble for that, but Hector had told Papa that it had been his idea, and Papa had whipped him even though he hadn't believed Hector for a second. "Hector . . ."

But his eyes fluttered closed. Lindy began to cry.

Chapter 28

AN HOUR LATER, LINDY was still sitting next to her brother's body, although she had moved just a few feet away so she could see around the building to the parking lot. Alex was directing the state police around the crime scene. Some of the shades lying near the parked cars had started to decompose: they'd either been shot multiple times or bled out before they could heal. Apparently the methamphetamine slowed that down as well, at least for brand-new shades.

The rest of the unconscious shades, Hector included, were now sporting wrists and ankles covered in zip ties, to prevent them from escaping if they woke up early. The state police were struggling to haul all the bodies into vans for transport. Lindy knew she should really get up and help them, but she wasn't letting Hector out of her sight for a second, not until he was in prison.

So she watched the action, and Alex called and texted frequently to give her updates and answer the questions she pushed into his head. Apparently, the remaining shades on the roof had vanished, along with Sloane and Reagan. Lindy had to kind of smile when Alex told her, picturing Reagan as the Pied Piper leading the new vampires away. Lindy wasn't worried about Reagan reneging on their arrangement: the young woman wasn't about to miss the opportunity to make real change. She would make sure the new shades disappeared into her little network of friends, and then she'd be back, with Sloane in tow.

Ruiz, Hadley, and Faraday had all been taken to the hospital, with a whole host of injuries that ranged from a three-inch scratch on Hadley's forearm to Faraday's chewed-up leg, which would probably require a blood transfusion. Noelle was at the hospital too, being treated for shock and the wound in her arm.

Only Alex and Chase remained, although the paramedics had really wanted to take Chase to the hospital too. He'd refused to leave until Alex did. Lindy intended to remedy that, so every few minutes she mentally nagged at Alex to get medical treatment. She planned to keep going until she wore him down.

Lindy heard someone approaching, and smelled Chase Eddy's aftershave as he came around the side of the building. He limped over to her and laboriously sat down on the ground next to her and Hector. He put her missing push dagger on the ground between them, sliding it over. "Found this on the roof. Figured you didn't want it processed into evidence."

"Thank you."

Neither of them said anything for a few minutes, watching Alex off in the distance.

"He's good at this," Chase observed. "I mean, I knew he was a good agent, but I wasn't sure how he would handle the bureaucracy stuff. He's doing great."

"He is," she agreed.

There was a brief pause, and then Chase said, "I haven't told him yet, but I've made a decision. Tomorrow morning I'm turning in my resignation."

For the first time, Lindy turned to look at him. Chase's arm was in a sling, and there were a lot of bandages padded on his shoulder. He looked pale and tired—but at peace. For maybe the first time since that night in Heavenly.

"It wasn't your fault, Chase," she said. "It could have been any of you."

"Not Alex."

"But Hector wanted Alex distracting me. He picked you because it would hurt Alex the most, and throw everyone off."

"Well, it worked," Chase said simply. "I can't be a federal agent anymore, Lindy. Not after all this. And especially not after Palmer."

She sighed. But then, she understood, too. "What will you do?"

"Go back to Arizona, by my folks. I've got a little savings; I'll take some time off, get to know my sister's fiancé. When I called to get them away from the house, just in case Hector sent someone, Kate told me she's two months pregnant. I want to be there for that."

"And then?"

He shrugged. "Maybe I'll join the local PD, maybe I'll find something else. But I'm done here. I'm done."

He said it with such finality, but Lindy could tell there was something else. She waited him out, and after a minute he glanced down at Hector.

"He's not going to stop, you know," Chase said quietly. "Even if he stays in Camp Vamp, he can do a lot of damage from the inside."

Lindy's insides felt heavy. "I know."

"But you didn't kill him."

She looked down at her brother. It would be so easy. He was unconscious, and restrained. "I can't," she said simply. "Maybe in the heat of battle, but not like this. Not in cold blood. He's my brother."

"Lindy." Chase met her eyes, and she saw there what he wanted her to know. A long, tense moment passed between them, and Lindy felt more tears spill down her cheeks. She made her decision and nodded.

Slowly, she stood up. "I think I'll see about pilfering some blood bags from that ambulance," she said, her voice only shaking a little. "Take care of yourself, Chase."

"Take care of Alex, okay?" His voice, too, was cracking.

She glanced back at him over her shoulder. "You have my word."

She began moving toward the group of cars. The little oasis of light had expanded exponentially, thanks to all the flashing police lights and ambulances. Alex was in the middle of them, looking exhausted. He glanced her way and smiled tiredly. She was definitely going to make him go to the hospital before he fell over.

Behind her, Lindy heard the metallic scratch of her push dagger being picked up off the pavement.

Epilogue

**THE HOOVER BUILDING, WASHINGTON, DC
TWO WEEKS LATER**

LINDY SAT IN THE small waiting area, flipping through an ancient magazine. She made a point to fidget a little: recrossing her legs, adjusting her new glasses. She was still getting used to both the glasses and her hair: now a rich dark red, cut just above her shoulders. It still surprised Lindy when she looked in a mirror, but she'd had to make that kind of adjustment many times before. She'd get used to it.

Finally, Alex strode down the hall toward her, buttoning his suit coat. The bruises from that night had faded almost completely. He looked good . . . but unhappy. Lindy stood up to meet him.

"So? What did Harding say?" she asked when he got close.

He leaned in to kiss her cheek and shrugged. "Two more weeks of suspension, reprimand in my file, basically a slap on the wrist. They're not even demoting me."

"You sound . . . disappointed."

"People died. If I had done things differently . . ."

She reached up and wrapped her arms around him. The night they'd first slept together, Lindy had worried that they'd have to hide any sort of relationship from everyone at work. Now that she was no longer Rosalind Frederick, though, nobody cared if she and Alex were together. It was nice. "Honestly, Alex? People were always going to die in apprehending Hector. Always. You did the best you could to minimize a necessary loss."

He gave her a startled look, one that Lindy had seen before. She'd just reminded him that she was a powerful shade and not a human girlfriend. She wasn't the only one making adjustments.

Alex gave a tiny, "agree to disagree" kind of shrug. "Did you get Reagan settled?" he asked, obviously ready to change the subject.

Lindy smiled. "Yes. She's got a nice apartment near the Capitol, and now she'll have plenty of money. As long as the media doesn't figure out her address, she should be able to live under the radar for a bit, testifying to Congress when she can." The entire world thought "Rosalind Frederick" had been responsible for Hector's death, and Reagan was getting more positive press as a result. No one was talking about arresting her for being a shade. "And Sloane seems very happy being her bodyguard."

"Do you think he'll ever tell her he loves her?" Alex mused.

She grinned. "I think Sloane would wait the next thousand years for Reagan to figure it out for herself."

Lindy took his arm, and they began walking back toward the parking garage. "So I've got two weeks before I can go back to work," he said.

"What do you want to do?" she asked.

"We could go somewhere," he suggested. "Someplace sandy, with really big beach umbrellas that are UV protected."

Lindy chuckled, but said, "I was thinking somewhere a little closer to home." It came out of her mouth before she'd considered it, but then, she supposed that was what Chicago was now. Home.

It was nice having a home. She was staying at Alex's apartment, but only until she sorted out having "Rosalind Frederick" sell the brownstone to her new identity, Lindsay Taylor.

"Oh, yeah?" Alex perked up. "What were you thinking?"

"Well . . . I promised Hadley I'd look into her brother's murder."

"Ah. A cold case."

"Yep. It was ten or twelve years ago, I believe. He was a cop, and she thinks shades might have been involved."

"And it'd have to be an off-the-books investigation," he mused. "Sounds right up our alley."

She brightened. "You wanna work a cold case with me?"

Alex kissed the top of her head. "Miss Taylor, I literally thought you'd never ask."

About the Author

Photograph by Elizabeth Craft

MELISSA F. OLSON has published eight novels in her Old World series for 47North, two novellas for Tor.com, and a standalone mystery. She spends most of her nonwriting professional time traveling around to conventions and conferences, where she speaks about issues related to genre, feminism, writing, and parenting.

Melissa lives in Madison, Wisconsin, with her husband, kids, pit bulls, and chinchillas.

TOR·COM

Science fiction. Fantasy. The universe.

And related subjects.

*

More than just a publisher's website, *Tor.com*

is a venue for **original fiction, comics,** and

discussion of the entire field of SF and fantasy,

in all media and from all sources. Visit our site

today—and join the conversation yourself.